Henry Francis Lyte

Miscellaneous poems

Henry Francis Lyte

Miscellaneous poems

ISBN/EAN: 9783337206277

Printed in Europe, USA, Canada, Australia, Japan

Cover: Foto ©Andreas Hilbeck / pixelio.de

More available books at **www.hansebooks.com**

MISCELLANEOUS POEMS

RIVINGTONS

London	*Waterloo Place.*
Oxford	*High Street.*
Cambridge	*Trinity Street.*

MISCELLANEOUS POEMS

BY HENRY FRANCIS LYTE, M.A.

LATE INCUMBENT OF LOWER BRIXHAM, DEVON

RIVINGTONS

London, Oxford, and Cambridge

1868

Preface

The continued demand for the Poems of the late Rev. Henry Francis Lyte (Author of the well-known Hymn 'Abide with me,' and of others which have found their way into almost every modern collection of Sacred Poetry), has induced the publishers to reprint the Miscellaneous Poems originally published in the two volumes, entitled 'POEMS, CHIEFLY RELIGIOUS,' and 'REMAINS OF THE REV. H. F. LYTE, WITH A PREFATORY MEMOIR' (one of his Prize Poems, entitled 'The Battle of Salamanca,' written while at Trinity College, Dublin, being alone omitted).

Should this volume meet with the success anticipated, it is proposed to publish the remaining Poems of the Author, including 'THE SPIRIT OF THE PSALMS,' in a second volume, uniform with the present, so as to form a complete collection of his Poetical Works.

September, 1868.

Contents

'How shall we sing the Lord's song in a strange land?'

THE song of God, so nobly sung
    By angels in a higher sphere,
Shall my unworthy heart and tongue
    Attempt its numbers here ?

With spirit cleaving to the dust,
    How should I hope to glow and soar ?
How speak of heavenly joy and trust,
    Till I have felt them more ?

A

An heir of guilt, a child of sin,
    An exile in a world like this,
What should I find without, within,
    To match with Him and His?

In vain I spread my flickering wings ;
    In vain I strive aloft to flee :
Great Lord of lords, and King of kings,
    I cannot sing of Thee !

I want a seraph's lofty voice,
    I want a seraph's soaring wing,
Before I make such themes my choice,
    And God's dread glories sing.

Thou needest not a note of mine
    To swell the triumphs of Thy throne,
Where myriads round Thee bend and shine,
    And Heaven is all Thy own !

No, rather let me sit and sigh,
    And drop contrition's silent tear :
Praise is the task of saints on high ;
    But prayer of sinners here.

The song of God, that glorious song,
    From me in such a world as this?
O no ! a worthier heart and tongue
    Must speak of Him and His.

Elijah's Interview with God

'And he said, Go forth, and stand upon the mount before the LORD. *And, behold, the* LORD *passed by, and a great and strong wind rent the mountains, and brake in pieces the rocks, before the* LORD; *but the* LORD *was not in the wind: and after the wind an earthquake; but the* LORD *was not in the earthquake: and after the earthquake a fire; but the* LORD *was not in the fire; and after the fire a still small voice.'*—1 KINGS xix. 11-12.

ON Horeb's rock the prophet stood :
   The LORD before him passed :
A hurricane in angry mood
   Swept by him strong and fast.
The forests fell before its force ;
The rocks were shivered in its course :
   God rode not in the blast !
"Twas but the whirlwind of His breath,
Announcing danger, wreck, and death.

It ceased : the air was mute.   A cloud
    Came muffling up the sun :
Went through the mountains deep and loud
    An earthquake thundered on.
The frighted eagle sprang in air ;
The wolf ran howling from his lair.
    God was not in the stun !
'Twas but the rolling of His car,
The trampling of His steeds from far.

It ceased again : and Nature stood
    And smoothed her ruffled frame :
When swift from heaven a fiery flood
    To earth devouring came.
Down to his depths the ocean fled ;
The sickening sun looked wan and dead.
    Yet God filled not the flame !
'Twas but the fierceness of His eye,
That lightened through the troubled sky.

At last a voice all still and small
   Rose sweetly on the ear ;
Yet rose so calm and clear that all
   In heaven and earth might hear.
It spoke of hope ; it spoke of love ;
It spoke as spirits speak above ;
   And God Himself was here !
For, oh, it was a Father's voice,
That bade His trembling world rejoice.

Speak, gracious LORD, speak ever thus ;
   And let Thy terrors prove
The harbingers of peace to us,
   The heralds of Thy love !
Shine through the earthquake, fire, and storm,
Shine in Thy milder, better form,
   And all our fears remove !
One word of Thine is all we claim ;
'Tis ' mercy ' through a Saviour's name.

The Mother and her Dying Boy

BOY

My mother, my mother, O let me depart!

Your tears and your pleadings are swords to
    my heart.

I hear gentle voices, that chide my delay;

I see lovely visions, that woo me away.

My prison is broken, my trials are o'er!

O mother, my mother, detain me no more!

MOTHER

And will you then leave us, my brightest, my
    best?

And will you run nestling no more to my breast?

The summer is coming to sky and to bower;

The tree that you planted will soon be in flower;

You loved the soft season of song and of bloom :
Oh, shall it return, and find you in the tomb?

BOY

Yes, mother, I loved in the sunshine to play,
And talk with the birds and the blossoms all
    day,
But sweeter the songs of the spirits on high,
And brighter the glories round God in the sky :
I see them! I hear them! they pull at my
    heart !
My mother, my mother, O let me depart !

MOTHER

O do not desert us ! Our hearts will be drear,
Our home will be lonely, when you are not here.
Your brother will sigh 'mid his playthings, and
    say,
I wonder dear Willie so long can delay.

That foot like the wild wind, that glance like a
    star—
O what will this world be, when they are afar?

BOY

This world, dearest mother! O live not for this;
No, press on with me to the fulness of bliss !
And, trust me, whatever bright fields I may roam,
My heart will not wander from you and from
    home.
Believe me still near you on pinions of love ;
Expect me to hail you when soaring above.

MOTHER

Well,—go, my beloved ! The conflict is o'er :—
My pleas are all selfish ; I urge them no more.
Why chain your bright spirit down here to the
    clod,
So thirsting for freedom, so ripe for its God ?

Farewell, then! farewell, till we meet at the
Throne,
Where love fears no partings, and tears are un-
known!

BOY

O Glory! O Glory! what music! what light!
What wonders break in on my heart, on my
sight!
I come, blessed spirits! I hear you from high.
O frail, faithless nature, can this be to die?
So near! what, so near to my Saviour and
King?
O help me, ye angels, His glories to sing!

The Alps

The Alps—the Alps—the joyous Alps,
    Are all around me heaving high.
I bow me to their snowy scalps,
    That rush into the sky.

Hail, lordly land of storm and strife,
    To poetry and wonder dear!
'Tis worth an age of common life
    To feel as I do here:

To look down on that deep-blue lake;
    To look up in that glorious sky;
To feel my soul within me wake,
    And ask for wings to fly:

To bound the airy heights along ;
  Above the floating clouds to stand ;
And meet Creation's God among
  The wonders of His hand.

Hail, scenes of holy grandeur ! hail !
  Where mortal sense stands hushed and awed.
Oh, who could gaze on such, and fail
  To think of Thee, my God ?

Alone and dread Thou dwellest here,
  The Source and Soul of all I see.
I look around in joy and fear,
  And feel I am with Thee !

I see Thee on the mountain sit,
  At summer's noon, sublime and still ;
Or, in the giant shadows flit
  Along from hill to hill.

I read Thy presence and Thy power
In each eternal rock I meet ;
I trace Thy love in every flower
That blossoms at my feet.

Thou speakest from each rolling cloud
That pours its stormy mirth on high,
When cliff to cliff is shouting loud,
Responsive to the sky.

Thy voice at night is in the sound
Of sinking glaciers, rushing rills,
And avalanches thundering round
Among the startled hills.

The mountain mists, in all their moods,
The snows by earthly feet untrod,
The fells, the forests, and the floods,
Are all instinct with God.

O regions, wonderful and wild,
    Sublimity's inspiring home,
Scenes I have dreamt of since a child,
    And longed as now to roam !

And I am here ! and I may range
    Your length and breadth without control
And feel a world all new and strange
    Break in upon my soul !

Hail, mountain monarchs ! hail !   Again
    Before your reverend feet I bow :
How poor is language to explain
    The thoughts that fill me now !

Mary's Grave

MARY, thou art gone to rest;
  Why should we deplore thee?
Light the turf lies on thy breast,
  Soft the winds breathe o'er thee.
Here within thy native clay
  Calmly thou art sleeping,
Safer, happier, far than they
  Who are o'er thee weeping.

Pleasant is thy lowly bed,
  Close to those that bore thee;
Trees, 'neath which thy childhood played,
  Gently waving o'er thee.

Hark the thrush ! how sweet his lay !
　　See the flowers, how blooming !
'Weep not for the dead,' they say,
　　''Though in earth consuming.

'Weep not for her—she is gone
　　Where no cares can move her ;
All her earthly labours done,
　　All her trials over.
Weep not—she has found a home
　　Where no sorrow paineth :
Sin, nor tears, nor terrors come,
　　Where a Saviour reigneth.'

'The Unknown God'

*'God, that made the world, and all things therein, seeing that He is Lord of heaven and earth, dwelleth not in temples made with hands.'—*ACTS *xvii.* 24

THE Lord hath builded for Himself;
    He needs no earthly dome :
The universe His dwelling is,
    Eternity His home.

Yon glorious sky His temple stands,
    So lofty, bright, and blue,
All lamped with stars, and curtained round
    With clouds of every hue.

Earth is His altar : nature there
    Her daily tribute pays :
The elements upon Him wait,
    The seasons roll His praise.

Where shall I see Him? How describe
  The Dread, Eternal One?
His foot-prints are in every place,
  Himself is found in none.

He called the world, and it arose;
  The heavens, and they appeared:
His hand poured forth the mighty deep;
  His arm the mountains reared.

He sets His foot upon the hills,
  And earth beneath Him quakes;
He walks upon the hurricane,
  And in the thunder speaks.

I search the rounds of space and time,
  Nor find His semblance there:
Grandeur has nothing so sublime,
  Nor beauty half so fair.

Yet all I am, or meet, proclaim
   His wisdom, love, and power :
They shine from all yon rolling worlds :
   They bloom in every flower.

He is ; He was ; He aye shall be.
   But how, my soul ? and what ?
Where is He ?—say, ye works of His —
   Vain thought ! where is He not ?

Thou Omnipresent, dread Unknown,
   Engage me evermore :
Enlarge my views, exalt my soul,
   And help me to adore !

Stability

There is a change in all below ;
  Nought sure beneath the sky :
Suns rise and set, tides ebb and flow,
  And man but lives to die.

Our joys and sorrows, hopes and fears,
  Still course each other on :
A blessing in our path appears—
  We grasp, and it is gone !

No drop of honey, but a sting
  Within it lies concealed ;
No hour that passes, but its wing
  Away some good has wheeled.

The joyous sun that lights to-day
But clouds to-morrow's sky :
The stars but shine to fall away ;
The world but lives to die.

And let them pass—each earthly thing
While, Lord, 't is mine to stand
On Thy eternal word, and cling
To Thy almighty hand.

Though sun and moon should sink in gloom,
Thy promise ne'er declines :
Dissolving worlds but leave Thee room
To work Thy vast designs.

Linked to Thy truth I hold me up,
Though earth from 'neath me slide ;
And take content whatever cup
Thy wisdom may provide.

Bitter or sweet, I little heed :
All, all is sweet to me,
While I my title clearly read
To joys at last with Thee.

On a Naval Officer buried in the Atlantic

THERE is, in the wide lone sea,
  A spot unmarked, but holy;
For there the gallant and the free
  In his ocean bed lies lowly.

Down, down, within the deep,
  That oft to triumph bore him,
He sleeps a sound and pleasant sleep,
  With the salt waves washing o'er him.

He sleeps serene, and safe
  From tempest or from billow,
Where the storms, that high above him chafe,
  Scarce rock his peaceful pillow.

The sea and him in death
They did not dare to sever :
It was his home while he had breath ;
  'T is now his rest for ever.

Sleep on, thou mighty dead !
A glorious tomb they 've found thee.
The broad blue sky above thee spread,
  The boundless waters round thee.

No vulgar foot treads here ;
No hand profane shall move thee ;
But gallant fleets shall proudly steer,
  And warriors shout, above thee.

And when the last trump shall sound,
And tombs are asunder riven,
Like the morning sun from the wave thou'lt
  bound,
  To rise and shine in heaven.

The Voice of God—*For Music*

PSALM XXIX.

GLORY and praise to Jehovah on high !
Glory from all, through the earth and the sky!
Angels, approach Him in homage and duty ;
　Fall at the feet of your Heavenly King :
Saints, to His presence O throng, in the beauty
　Of holy devotion His mercies to sing.
　Glory and praise to Jehovah on high !
　Glory from all, through the earth and the sky!

　The voice of Jehovah, majestic and loud,
　In thunders comes forth from his palace of
　　cloud ;
That voice o'er the silence of ocean is breaking :
It rolls o'er the waters, it bursts on the shore :

The forests are bending, the mountains are
    quaking,
  And earth and her creatures stand still and
    adore.
  Glory and praise to Jehovah on high!
  Glory from all, through the earth and the sky!

The voice of Jehovah more sweetly is heard
By saints in His temple attending His word.
He speaks not to them in the whirlwind or
    thunder;
  He comes not to threaten, denounce, or
    reprove:
He comes with glad tidings of joy and of
    wonder;
  He bids them be blest in Immanuel's love.
  Glory and praise to Jehovah on high!
  Glory from all, through the earth and the sky!

Agnes

I saw her in childhood—
A bright gentle thing,
Like the dawn of the morn,
Or the dews of the spring :
The daisies and hare-bells
Her playmates all day ;
Herself as light-hearted
And artless as they.

I saw her again—
A fair girl of eighteen,
Fresh glittering with graces
Of mind and of mien.

Her speech was all music ;
   Like moonlight she shone :
The envy of many,
   The glory of one.

Years, years fleeted over-
   I stood at her foot :
The bud had grown blossom,
   The blossom was fruit.
A dignified mother,
   Her infant she bore ;
And looked, I thought, fairer
   Than ever before.

I saw her once more—
   "T was the day that she died .
Heaven's light was around her,
   And God at her side ;

No wants to distress her,
No fears to appal—
O then, I felt, then
She was fairest of all !

The Approach of Spring

O ! SPRING-TIME now will soon be here----
The sweetest time of all the year ;
When fields are green, and skies are blue,
And the world grows beautiful anew.

The storms and clouds shall pass from high ;
And the sun walk lordly up the sky,
And look down love and joy again
On herb, and beast, and living men.

Then the laughing flowers on plant and tree
Shall bud and blossom pleasantly ;
And spirits through the buxom air
Drop health and gladness every where :

The birds shall build their nests, and wake
Their roundelays in bush and brake;
And the young west-wind on joyous feet
Go wooing along from sweet to sweet.

Then lives lithe Hope, live Love and Mirth;
Then God in beauty walks the earth:
The heart is in tune, and the life-blood plays,
And the soul breaks out in songs of praise.

O! spring-time now will soon be here,
The sweetest time of all the year;
When green leaves burst, and flow'rets spring,
And young hearts too are blossoming.

'T was then I ventured first to twine
My Annie's trembling arm in mine;
And trod—with her I cared not where—
Through vocal fields and scented air.

O days of sunshine, song, and flowers !
O young Love's early haunts and hours !
O tones and looks ! O smiles and tears !
How shine ye still through lapse of years !

There was one bank we loved to climb,
All matted o'er with fragrant thyme,
And screened from every vagrant breeze
But the sweet south, up which the bees

Came musical ; and there we stood,
And gazed down on the ocean flood,
That slept beneath us heaving mild
Between his shores, like a cradled child ;

Or turned where on the orchard trees
Young Spring sat swinging in the breeze,
Unfolding buds, and tending flowers,
For Summer's future fruits and bowers.

All, all was bright !—at times like this
No sight or sound comes in amiss ;
But things around appear to win
A colour from the mood within.

The earth laughed into flower : the sky
Cleared off the cloud from its brow on high ;
And God—the God of grace—unfurled
His flag of peace o'er a fallen world.

These youthful days are past and gone ;
The autumn of my years comes on ;
I much am changed in mind and frame ;
Yet Spring, sweet Spring, comes still the same.

I grow young with the young year then ;
I live my past lot o'er again ;
And in these hours of song and bloom
See types of those beyond the tomb.

O ! spring-time now will soon be here,
The spring of Heaven's millennial year ;
When God again o'er nature's night,
Shall say, ' Be light,' and there is light.

O Thou that into glorious birth
Shalt wake at last this fallen earth,
While humbler things Thy influence share,
Be not the soul forgotten there !

Rise, Sun of Glory ! rise, and shine
Within this wintry breast of mine ;
And make my inward wastes and snows
Rejoice and blossom as the rose.

Oh, while I seem to catch the sound
Of vegetation swelling round,
Grant me within a growth to prove
Of faith, and hope, and joy, and love !

Spring-tide of grace, thy course begin ;
Chase the dark reign of sense and sin ;
From light to light advance and shine,
'Till Heaven's eternal spring is mine !

Nobember

THE autumn wind is moaning low the requiem
    of the year ;
The days are growing short again, the fields
    forlorn and sere ;
The sunny sky is waxing dim, and chill the
    hazy air ;
And tossing trees before the breeze are turning
    brown and bare.

All nature and her children now prepare for
    rougher days :
The squirrel makes his winter bed, and hazel
    hoard purveys ;

The sunny swallow spreads his wing to seek a
    brighter sky;
And boding owl, with nightly howl, says cloud
    and storm are nigh.

No more 't is sweet to walk abroad among the
    evening dews:
The flowers are fled from every path, with all
    their scents and hues:
The joyous bird no more is heard, save where
    his slender song
The robin drops, as meek he hops the withered
    leaves among.

Those withered leaves, that slender song, a
    solemn truth convey,—
In wisdom's ear they speak aloud of frailty and
    decay:
They say that man's apportioned year shall
    have its winter too;
Shall rise and shine, and then decline, as all
    around him do.

They tell him, all he has on earth, his brightest
    dearest things,
His loves and friendships, joys and hopes, have
    all their falls and springs :
A wave upon a moon-lit sea, a leaf before the
    blast,
A summer flower, an April hour, that gleams
    and hurries past.

And be it so : I know it well : myself, and all
    that's mine,
Must roll on with the rolling year, and ripen to
    decline.
I do not shun the solemn truth : to him it is
    not drear
Whose hopes can rise above the skies, and see
    a Saviour near.

It only makes him feel with joy, this earth is
  not his home ;
It sends him on from present ills to brighter
  hours to come :
It bids him take with thankful heart whate'er
  his God may send,
Content to go through weal or woe to glory in
  the end.

Then murmur on, ye wintry winds ; remind me
  of my doom :
Ye lengthened nights, still image forth the
  darkness of the tomb.
Eternal summer lights the heart where Jesus
  deigns to shine.
I mourn no loss, I shun no cross, so thou,
  O Lord, art mine !

'Lo, we have left all, and followed Thee'

Jesus, I my cross have taken,
    All to leave and follow Thee :
Destitute, despised, forsaken,
    Thou from hence my all shalt be.
Perish, every fond ambition,
    All I 've sought, and hoped, and known ;
Yet how rich is my condition,—
    God and heaven are still my own !

Let the world despise and leave me—
    They have left my Saviour too—
Human hearts and looks deceive me ;
    Thou art not, like man, untrue :

And while Thou shalt smile upon me,
   God of wisdom, love, and might,
Foes may hate, and friends may shun me :
   Show Thy face, and all is bright !

Go then, earthly fame and treasure !
   Come, disaster, scorn, and pain !
In Thy service, pain is pleasure ;
   With thy favour, loss is gain.
I have called Thee Abba, Father ;
   I have stayed my heart on Thee :
Storms may howl, and clouds may gather ;
   All must work for good to me.

Man may trouble and distress me ;
   'T will but drive me to Thy breast.
Life with trials hard may press me ;
   Heaven will bring me sweeter rest.

Oh, 't is not in grief to harm me !
  While Thy love is left to me !
Oh, 't were not in joy to charm me,
  Were that joy unmixed with Thee.

Take, my soul, thy full salvation ;
  Rise o'er sin, and fear, and care ;
Joy to find in every station
  Something still to do or bear !
Think what Spirit dwells within thee ;
  What a Father's smile is thine ;
What thy Saviour died to win thee,—
  Child of Heaven, shouldst thou repine ?

Haste then on from grace to glory,
  Armed by faith, and winged by prayer ;
Heaven's eternal day 's before thee ;
  God's own hand shall guide thee there.

Soon shall close thy earthly mission ;
Swift shall pass thy pilgrim days ;
Hope soon change to glad fruition,
Faith to sight, and prayer to praise.

Morning Thoughts

Again, O Lord, I ope my eyes,
  Thy glorious light to see,
And share the gifts so largely lent
  To thankless man by Thee.

And why has God o'er me this night
  The watch so kindly kept?
And why have I so safely waked?
  And why so sweetly slept?

And wherefore do I live and breathe?
  And wherefore have I still
The mind to know, the sense to choose,
  The strength to do Thy will?

Is it, to waste another day
In folly, sin, and shame?
To give to these my heart and hand,
And spurn my Maker's claim?

Is it, for honour, wealth, or power
My heavenly hopes to sell?
Is it, to grasp at pleasure's flower
Upon the brink of hell?

Is it, to grow unto the world,
As glides the world from me;
Be one day nearer to the grave,
And further, Lord, from Thee?

No! thus too many days I've spent!
To Thee, then, this be given:
Teach what I owe to man below,
And to Thyself in heaven.

Oh, bring me to my Saviour's cross
For mercy for the past ;
And make me live the coming day
As if it were my last !

Evening

Sweet evening hour! sweet evening hour!
That calms the air, and shuts the flower;
That brings the wild bird to her nest,
The infant to its mother's breast.

Sweet hour! that bids the labourer cease;
That gives the weary team release,
And leads them home, and crowns them there
With rest and shelter, food and care.

O season of soft sounds and hues,
Of twilight walks among the dews,
Of feelings calm, and converse sweet,
And thoughts too shadowy to repeat!

The weeping eye, that loathes the day,
Finds peace beneath thy soothing sway;
And faith and prayer o'ermastering grief,
Burst forth, and bring the heart relief.

Yes, lovely hour! thou art the time
When feelings flow, and wishes climb;
When timid souls begin to dare,
And God receives and answers prayer.

Then trembling through the dewy skies
Look out the stars, like thoughtful eyes
Of angels, calm reclining there,
And gazing on this world of care.

Then, as the earth recedes from sight,
Heaven seems to ope her fields of light,
And call the fettered soul above,
From sin and grief, to peace and love.

Sweet hour! for heavenly musing made—
When Isaac walked, and Daniel prayed;
When Abram's offering God did own;
And Jesus loved to be alone.

Who has not felt that Evening's hour
Draws forth devotion's tenderest power;
That guardian spirits round us stand,
And God himself seems most at hand?

The very birds cry shame on men,
And chide their selfish silence, then:
The flowers on high their incense send;
And earth and heaven unite and blend.

Let others hail the rising day:
I praise it when it fades away;
When life assumes a higher tone,
And God and heaven are all my own.

Invocation

ALTERED FROM QUARLES

SPIRITS of light and love, who pace around
  The city's sapphire walls; whose stainless
    feet
Measure the gem-paved paths of sacred
    ground,
  And trace the New Jerusalem's jasper street!
Ah you, whose overflowing hearts are crowned
  With your best wishes; who enjoy the sweet
Of all your hopes; when next ye come before
My absent Lord, O say how I implore
From His reviving eye one look of kindness
    more.

Tell Him, O tell Him, how my widowed breast
  Beneath the burden of His frown has pined:

Tell Him, O tell Him, how I lie oppressed
  In all the tempest of a troubled mind.
O tell Him, tell Him, I can know no rest
  Till He shall smile, as once, appeased and
    kind.
Tell Him, I think upon the vows he sware—
His love, His truth, His grace—and thus I dare
To come before Him now with penitence and
  prayer.

Say, the parched soil desires not so the shower
  To quicken and refresh her embryo grain;
Say, the fallen crestlet of the drooping flower
  Wooes not the bounty of the genial rain,
As my lorn spirit looks out for the hour
  When her lost Lord shall visit her again.
Then, gentle spirits, should ye hear your lays,
And seem to melt, your best Hosannahs raise;
And with your heavenly notes sustain my feeble
  praise.

'Return unto Me, and I will return unto Thee'

Wilt Thou return to me, O Lord,
   If I return to Thee?
O Heavenly truth! O gracious word!
   My Hope and Refuge be!

Since from Thy foot I dared to roam,
   My soul has found no rest,
Chastised and contrite, back I come,
   To seek it in Thy breast.

And dost Thou say Thou wilt receive,
   And call me still Thy own?
My spirit, hear, accept, believe!
   And melt my heart of stone!

Again that gracious word to me !
  O speak that word again !
My guilt is pardoned ?—can it be ?—
  And loosed my every chain ?

No, blessed Lord ; not every chain,
  Not every bond, remove :
Let one, at least, unloosed remain—
  The bond of grateful love.

𝕱𝖑𝖞, 𝖞𝖊 𝕳𝖔𝖚𝖗𝖘—*For Music*

FLY, ye hours, the best, the brightest :
Best are they that fleet the lightest !
Man, be wise :
Thy earthly joys
Are poor, compared with those thou slightest.

The world we roam
Is not our home :
We seek a rest that aye remaineth.
Through weal or woe,
From all below
We haste to scenes where nothing paineth.
Fly, ye hours, etc.

It is not life,

This toil and strife :

These only serve from God to sever.

We hope to rise

Above the skies ;

And there shall live, and live for ever.

                    Fly, ye hours, etc.

Can that be gain,

Whose charms detain

The soul from glory's richer treasures !

Can that be woe,

That serves to throw

A brighter hue o'er coming pleasures !

Fly, ye hours, the best, the brightest !

Thou that in the world delightest,

Rise, O rise

To nobler joys ;

And taste the bliss which now thou slightest.

'Whither shall I fly from Thy presence?'

Where shall I fly? What dark untrodden path
Will lead a sinner from his Maker's wrath?
Alas! where'er I bend my outcast way,
His eye can search, His mighty hand hath sway.

Is there no island in the depths of space,
No distant world, where I may shun His chase?
Ah no!   Of all He is the spring and soul:
All feel His care, all own His high control.

But there is night :—perhaps her murky womb
May wrap and hide me in its depths of gloom?
No: He that says, ' Be light, and there is light,'
Can look Omniscience thro' the dunnest night.

Give me then morning's wings: I'll fling me
   where
The desert waste ne'er claims His eye or care.
Vain hope! If He were absent, conscience
   then
Would act the God, and scare me back to men.

Well, then, the ocean : she my head shall hide,
And quench His bolts in her o'ersheltering tide.
Fool! the dark waves cleave wide at His com-
   mand ;
And, lo, He walks them as He walks the land.

What say the rocks? Stern marble, ope thy
   breast,
And lock me in to monumental rest.
Vain, vain! His voice the rocks have often
   heard ;
Nay, worlds dissolve before His lightest word.

Be death then mine! At least the grave, or hell,
Will yield some sullen nook where I may dwell.
No: the last trump shall burst the bars of death;
And God's stern presence felt makes hell beneath.

Where then to flee? how shun His arm, His eye?
Where find what earth, and heaven, and hell
    deny?
How pass beyond His infinite patrol,
Who fills, pervades, informs the mighty whole!

O where to flee? There is but one retreat—
'T is that which brings me contrite to His feet:
A change of heart, and not a change of place,
That flees from Justice to the arms of Grace.

The Saviour calls: 'Come, trembler, to My
    breast;
' Beneath My cross thou may'st securely rest:
' Washed in My blood, thy guilt will all remove;
' And wrath eternal grow Eternal Love.'

Autumnal Hymn

The leaves around me falling
  Are preaching of decay ;
The hollow winds are calling,
  ' Come, pilgrim, come away !'
The day, in night declining,
  Says, I must too decline :
The year its life resigning—
  Its lot foreshadows mine.

The light my path surrounding,
  The loves to which I cling,
The hopes within me bounding,
  The joys that round me wing—

All melt like stars of even,
 Before the morning's ray
Pass upward into heaven,
 And chide at my delay.

The friends gone there before me
 Are calling me from high,
And joyous angels o'er me
 Tempt sweetly to the sky.
'Why wait,' they say, 'and wither
 ''Mid scenes of death and sin?
'O rise to glory hither,
 'And find true life begin!'

I hear the invitation,
 And fain would rise and come—
A sinner, to salvation;
 An exile, to his home:

But while I here must linger,
Thus, thus, let all I see
Point on, with faithful finger,
To heaven, O Lord, and Thee.

Parted Christians

When reft of the converse of those that they love,
  The godless may fret and repine :
"'T is ours to look up to a Father above,
  And try to His will to resign.
The friends in a Saviour need not be deplored,
  Wherever their lot may be cast :
Tho' severed on earth, we are one in the Lord,
  And shall meet in His presence at last.

Our Guardian all-wise and all-merciful is ;
  He knows, and will give us, the best :
Assured we shall still be each other's and His,
  To Him we relinquish the rest.

We each commend each to Omnipotent hands,
  And calm on His promise repose ;
And know that, though scattered o'er seas and
    o'er lands,
  We are sure to reach home at the close.

Meanwhile, we kneel down at the same Throne
    of Grace ;
  We breathe up the same daily prayer ;
We march the same road to the same happy
    place,
  The same Spirit guiding us there.
Sweet hope realizes the things that shall be,
  And memory those that have been ;
And, reaching by these to what sense cannot see,
  We lose the dark present between.

We strive to be all that the absent would love ;
  To flee from what they would condemn ;

Intent, when we meet, upon earth or above.
To be found the more worthy of them.
With aims so exalted, and trust so secure,
All else is in lovely accord,
All holy, all happy, all peaceful and pure.—
Oh, who would not love in the Lord?

Ellen

SHE rests beneath her native earth,
Close to the spot that gave her birth.
Her young feet trod the flowers that bloom—
Meet emblems—on her early tomb :
Her living voice was wont to cheer
The echoes which our sorrows hear.

She rests beneath her native earth ;
And few remain to speak her worth.
Her little sojourn here was spent
In unobtrusive banishment :
A flower upon the desert thrown,
That lived and breathed to God alone.

Yet long her gentle ways shall dwell
In hearts that knew and loved her well;
And oft they lift their tearful eyes,
To hear her calling from the skies;
And ill could they her absence bear,
But that they hope to join her there.

Spare my Flower

O SPARE my flower, my gentle flower,
  The slender creature of a day!
Let it bloom out its little hour,
  And pass away.
Too soon its fleeting charms must lie
  Decayed, unnoticed, overthrown.
O hasten not its destiny,—
  Too like thy own.

The breeze will roam this way to-morrow,
  And sigh to find his playmate gone:
The bee will come its sweets to borrow,
  And meet with none.

O spare ! and let it still outspread
Its beauties to the passing eye,
And look up from its lowly bed
Upon the sky.

O spare my flower !   Thou know'st not what
Thy undiscerning hand would tear :
A thousand charms thou notest not
Lie treasured there.
Not Solomon, in all his state,
Was clad like nature's simplest child ;
Nor could the world combined create
One floweret wild.

Spare then this humble monument
Of an Almighty's power and skill ;
And let it at His shrine present
Its homage still.

He made it who makes nought in vain :
He watches it who watches thee ;
And He can best its date ordain
Who bade it be.

O spare my flower—for it is frail ;
A timid, weak, imploring thing—
And let it still upon the gale
Its moral fling.
That moral thy reward shall be :
Catch the suggestion, and apply :—
' Go, live like me,' it cries ; ' like me
' Soon, soon to die.'

Aspirations

I WOULD not always sail
Upon a sunny sea :
The mountain wave, the sounding gale,
Have deeper joys for me.

Let others love to creep
Along the flowery dell :
Be mine upon the craggy steep,
Among the storms, to dwell.

The rock, the mist, the foam,
The wonderful, the wild—
I feel they form my proper home.
And claim me for their child.

The whirlwind's rushing wing,
The stern volcano's voice,
To me an awful rapture bring :
I tremble and rejoice.

I love thy solemn roar,
Thou deep, eternal sea,
Sounding along from shore to shore
The boundless and the free.

I love the flood's hoarse song,
The thunder's lordly mirth,
The midnight wind, that walks along
The hushed and trembling earth ;

The mountain, lone and high.
The dark and silent wood,
The desert stretched from sky to sky
In awful solitude.

A presence and a power
In scenes like these I see :
The stillness of a midnight hour
Has eloquence for me.

Then, bursting earth's control,
My thoughts are all at flood :
I feel the stirrings in my soul
Of an immortal mood.

My energies expand ;
My spirit looks abroad ;
And, midst the terrible and grand,
Feels nearer to her God.

Let others tamely weigh
The danger and the pain :
I do not shrink the price to pay,
To share the joy and gain.

Winter

The billowy shore is booming loud,
The sky is black with storm and cloud,
The fields are bare, the air is chill,
And winter reigns from vale to hill.

The shortening day, the muffled sky,
The wild wind whistling bleakly by,
The naked fields, the leafless tree,
Speak, mortal man, speak all to thee.

They talk of sin, they talk of woe,
Of ruin wrought to all below:
They taunt the author of their doom,
And point him onward to the tomb.

The waves lift up their voice ; the woods
Make solemn answer to the floods :
They bid us stand abased and awed,
And own an Omnipresent God.

Calm on the tempest's hurrying wings
He walks His trembling earth, and flings,
Unmoved by elemental din,
His scourges o'er a world of sin.

Almighty ! be it mine to lie
Adoring as Thou passest by,
And hear Thee at the close proclaim
The gentler glories of Thy name !

The fire, the earthquake, and the wind—
In these my God I would not find—
But in the Voice still, small, and dim,
That speaks of Christ, and peace through Him.

'My Beloved is mine, and I am his'

IMITATED FROM QUARLES

Long did I toil, and knew no earthly rest ;
 Far did I rove, and found no certain home :
At last I sought them in His sheltering breast,
 Who opes His arms, and bids the weary come.
With Him I found a home, a rest divine ;
And I since then am His, and He is mine.

Yes, He is mine ! and nought of earthly things,
 Not all the charms of pleasure, wealth, or
  power,
The fame of heroes, or the pomp of kings,
 Could tempt me to forego His love an hour.
Go, worthless world, I cry, with all that 's thine !
Go ! I my Saviour's am, and He is mine.

The good I have is from His stores supplied:
The ill is only what He deems the best.
He for my friend, I 'm rich with nought beside ;
And poor without Him, though of all pos-
sessed.
Changes may come—I take, or I resign,
Content, while I am His, while He is mine.

Whate'er may change, in Him no change is seen,
A glorious sun, that wanes not, nor declines :
Above the clouds and storms He walks serene,
And on His people's inward darkness shines.
All may depart—I fret not nor repine,
While I my Saviour's am, while He is mine.

He stays me falling ; lifts me up when down ;
Reclaims me wandering ; guards from every
foe ;
Plants on my worthless brow the victor's crown,
Which in return before His feet I throw,

Grieved that I cannot better grace His shrine
Who deigns to own me His, as He is mine.

While here, alas ! I know but half His love,
  But half discern Him, and but half adore ;
But when I meet Him in the realms above,
  I hope to love Him better, praise Him more.
And feel, and tell, amid the choir divine,
How fully I am His, and He is mine.

A Summer Day in Winter

The winter wears a summer hue—
   The sun is on the wave;
The sky is one unclouded blue;
   The winds begin to rave;

The feathery frost melts fast away
   From every glittering stem;
And cottage eaves in morning's ray
   Are dropping gold and gem.

That ray the silver feet unlocks,
   Of all the tiny floods;
They leap again down o'er their rocks,
   And prattle through the woods.

The cattle in the field rejoice,
  The birds upon the wing,
And from the brake a doubtful voice
  Half warbles, Welcome Spring!

The wave that flew o'er yester cliff,
  Is sleeping 'neath it now;
And from its creek the summer skiff
  Steals out with timid prow.

The anchored ships, their voyage o'er,
  Shake out their sails to dry;
The fisher spreads his nets on shore,
  Beneath the glowing sky.

The old man from his chimney nook
  Creeps out into the sun:
All Nature wears her own sweet look
  Of spring-tide just begun.

O earth, all fallen as thou art,
How soon thy darkest day
Can into life and beauty start
Beneath thy monarch's ray!

Nor less the contrast that awakes
The wintry soul within,
When, Lord, thy gladdening Gospel breaks
On nature's night of sin.

The Sun of Righteousness ascends;
The clouds and storms depart;
And heaven-born Grace implants and tends
Her Eden in the heart.

Yet earth's best joys are brief and base
To those which Heaven supplies;
A summer smile on winter's face,
A gleam through clouded skies.

I would not spurn these wayside flowers,
　　That strew my pathway home ;
But look through all to heavenly hours.
　　And bid their fulness come.

'𝔍𝔢𝔰𝔲𝔰 𝔚𝔢𝔭𝔱'

ENLARGED FROM BEDDOME

DID Christ o'er sinners weep?
    And shall our cheeks be dry?
Let floods of penitential grief
    Burst forth from every eye.

The Son of God in tears
    The angels wondering see:
Hast thou no wonder, O my soul?
    He shed those tears for thee!

He wept that we might weep,
    Might weep our sin and shame;
He wept to show His love for us,
    And bid us love the same.

Then tender be our hearts,
Our eyes in sorrow dim,
'Till every tear from every eye
Is wiped away by Him!

Psalm cxxxix.

Omniscient God, Thine eye divine
My inmost soul can see ;
And every thought and act of mine
Is open, Lord, to Thee !

When up I rise, when down I lie,
Still Thou art at my side.
Where shall I shun Thy awful eye,
Or from Thy Spirit hide ?

If up to Heaven my flight I take,
I meet Thee face to face :
If down to Hell, Thy terrors make
The darkness of the place.

I plunge into the shades of night ;
But Thou art there with me :
And darkness kindles into light
Before one glance from Thee.

From Thee, O Lord, I came at first,
  The creature of Thy hand :
Thy providence my life has nursed,
  And by Thy grace I stand.

Each member of my wondrous frame
  Displays Thy skill and power;
And countless benefits proclaim
  Thy love from hour to hour.

Down in Thy arms at night I lie ;
  Thou watchest while I sleep.
I wake at morn ; Thou still art nigh,
  My soul to tend and keep.

Search me, O Lord ! my spirit prove,
  From sin O set me free !
And make my heart return the love
  It daily shares from Thee.

The Wall-flower

Why loves my flower, so high reclined
  Upon these walls of barren gloom,
To waste her sweetness on the wind,
  And far from every eye to bloom?
Why joy to twine with golden braid
This ruined rampart's aged head,
Proud to expose her gentle form,
And swing her bright locks in the storm?

That lonely spot is bleak and hoar,
  Where prints my flower her fragrant kiss;
Yet sorrow hangs not fonder o'er
  The ruins of her faded bliss.

And wherefore will she thus inweave
The owl's lone couch, and feel at eve
The wild bat o'er her blossoms fling,
And strike them down with heedless wing?

Thus, gazing on the loftiest tower
   Of ruined Fore at eventide,
The Muse addressed a lonely flower
   That bloomed above in summer pride.
The Muse's eye, the Muse's ear,
Can more than others see and hear:
The breeze of evening murmured by,
And gave, she deemed, this faint reply:

' On this lone tower, so wild and drear,
   ' 'Mid storms and clouds I love to lie,
' Because I find a freedom here
   ' Which prouder haunts could ne'er supply.

' Safe on these walls I sit, and stem
' The elements that conquered them ;
' And high o'er reach of plundering foe
' Smile on an anxious world below.

' Though envied place I may not claim
    ' On warrior's crest, or lady's hair ;
' Though tongue may never speak my name,
    ' Nor eye behold and own me fair ;
' To Him, who tends me from the sky,
' I spread my beauties here on high,
' And bid the winds to waft above
' My incense to His throne of love.

' And though in hermit solitude,
    ' Aloft and wild, my home I choose,
' On the rock's bosom pillowed rude,
    ' And nurtured by the falling dews ;

' Yet duly with the opening year

' I hang my golden mantle here.

' A child of God's I am, and He

' Sustains, and clothes, and shelters me.

' Nor deem my state without its bliss :

  ' Mine is the first young smile of day ;

' Mine the light zephyr's earliest kiss ;

  ' And mine the skylark's matin lay.

' These are my joys : with these on high

' In peace I hope to live and die,

' And drink the dew, and scent the breeze,

' As blithe a flower as Flora sees.'

Bloom on, sweet moralist !   Be thine

  The softest shower, the brightest sun !

Long o'er a world of error shine,

  And teach them what to seek and shun !

Bloom on, and show the simple glee
That dwells with those who dwell like thee ;
From noise, and glare, and folly driven,
To thought, retirement, peace, and heaven.

Show them, in thine, the Christian's lot,
  So dark and drear in worldly eyes ;
And yet he would exchange it not
  For all they most pursue and prize.
From meaner cares and trammels free,
He soars above the world, like thee ;
And, fed and nurtured from above,
Returns the debt in grateful love.

Frail, like thyself, fair flower, is he,
  And beat by every storm and shower ;
Yet on a Rock he stands, like thee,
  And braves the tempest's wildest power.

And there he blooms, and gathers still
A good from every seeming ill ;
And, pleased with what his lot has given,
He lives to God, and looks to heaven.

Jehovah-Jireh

WHEN earthly joys glide swift away,
   When hopes and comforts flee,
When foes beset, and friends betray,
   I turn, my God, to Thee !

Thy nature, Lord, no change can know ;
   Thy promise still is sure ;
And ills can ne'er so hopeless grow
   But Thou canst find a cure.

Deliverance comes most bright and blest
   At danger's darkest hour ;
And man's extremity is best
   To prove Almighty power.

High as Thou art, Thou still art near
When suppliants succour crave ;
And as Thine ear is swift to hear,
Thy arm is strong to save.

The Pilgrim's Progress

' Blessed is he whose transgression is forgiven, whose sin is covered.'—Psalm xxxii.

Blest is the broken, bleeding heart,
  For sin constrained to ache !
Soon Heavenly Hands shall bind it up,
  No more to bleed or break.

Blest are the eyes, whose burning tears
  O'er past transgressions fall !
The Sun of Righteousness shall rise,
  To dry, or light them all.

That broken heart, that tearful eye,
  That pensive pilgrim guise,
Are Heaven's own gifts, and more than all
  That worldlings seek or prize.

Who has them, claims and titles has
  Which none beside can own ;
Pledges of more than eye hath seen,
  Or heart conceived or known.

Through clouds and sunshine, storm and calm
  He on to glory goes,
With hope to light him o'er his way,
  And bliss to crown its close.

The wise may slight, the proud may shun !
  His God is with him still,
And adds a zest to all his joys,
  And lightens every ill.

Through Him he daily triumphs gains
  O'er Satan, self, and sin ;
Through Him new blessings smile without,
  New joy and peace within.

A coal from heaven has touched his lips,
   And filled his mouth with song;
And Faith and Love spring forth to waft
   His fainting steps along.

He goes, he goes, his fadeless crown
   From Christ's own hand to win!
The angels throng round heaven's high gate,
   To hail the stranger in!

The silver cord is loosed at last,
   The fettered soul takes wing;
Assumes its station fast by God,
   His ceaseless praise to sing.

The Pilgrim's Song

' There remaineth a rest for the people of God.'—HEB iv.

My rest is in heaven ; my rest is not here ;

Then why should I murmur when trials are near ?

Be hushed, my dark spirit ! the worst that can
 come

But shortens thy journey, and hastens thee home.

It is not for me to be seeking my bliss

And building my hopes in a region like this :

I look for a city which hands have not piled ;

I pant for a country by sin undefiled.

The thorn and the thistle around me may grow :

I would not lie down upon roses below :

I ask not my portion, I seek not a rest,

Till I find them, O Lord, in Thy sheltering breast.

Afflictions may damp me, they cannot destroy;
One glimpse of Thy love turns them all into joy:
And the bitterest tears, if Thou smile but on
    them,
Like dew in the sunshine, grow diamond and
    gem.

Let doubt then, and danger, my progress oppose;
They only make heaven more sweet at the close.
Come joy, or come sorrow, whate'er may befal,
An hour with my God will make up for it all.

A scrip on my back, and a staff in my hand,
I march on in haste through an enemy's land:
The road may be rough, but it cannot be long;
And I'll smooth it with hope, and I'll cheer it
    with song.

To a Blade of Grass

Poor little twinkler in the sun,
That liftest here thy modest head
For every breeze to blow upon,
And every passing foot to tread;

The loneliest waste, the humblest bower,
Content in homely green to dress,
And wear away thy little hour
In meek unheeded usefulness;

No hues of thine attract the eye,
No sweets allure the roving bee,
Nor deigns the dainty butterfly
To rest his wing on lowly thee.

All undistinguished and forgot
    Among the myriads of thy kind,
The moral of thy tranquil lot
    Thou wastest on the idle wind.

Be mine, while others pass thee by,
    To win and wear thee in my strain ;
And from thy gentle teaching try
    A lesson for my heart to gain.

While brighter children of the sun
    With altering seasons droop and die,
I see thee green and gladsome run
    Through all the changes of the sky.

Where vegetative life begins
    Thy little flag is first unfurled,
And marks the empire Nature wins
    From desolation round the world.

Yes; Nature claims thee for her own;
　Her thousand children house with thee:
An insect world, to eye unknown,
　Peoples thy coverts blithe and free.

The partridge, 'midst her speckled brood,
　Leans upon thee her cowering breast;
Thou giv'st the field-mouse home and food;
　Thou curtain'st round the sky-lark's nest.

Thou feed'st the honest steer by day,
　Thou strew'st at night his open bed;
The young lamb, in his morning play,
　Strikes down the dew-drop from thy head.

Oh, ever pleasing, ever plain,
　Creation's goodly household vest!
By thee is fringed the ruined fane,
　By thee the poor man's grave is drest.

The pilgrim of the sandy waste,
   The roamer of the long, long sea,
The sick-room's or the dungeon's guest—
   'T is his, 't is his, to value thee.

Green soother of the burning eye,
   Thou speak'st of sweet and simple things-
Of freedom, health, and purity,
   And all that buxom Nature brings.

Be mine to dwell with her, with thee ;
   At eventide the fields to roam ;
My God among His works to see,
   And call my wandering spirit home :

And, while I view the Hand, that tends
   Ten thousand worlds, so kind to thee,
To feel that He, who so descends,
   Will not o'erlook a worm like me.

A Fallen Sister

' The maid is not dead, but sleepeth '

SHE is not dead—she only sleeps :

Life in her soul its vigil keeps :

Though dark the cloud, though strong the chain.

Speak, Lord, and she shall live again !

She is not dead :—it cannot be

That one, whose soul so glowed to Thee,

Should all that's past renounce, forget :

Oh, speak, and she will hear Thee yet.

I know, I know how once she felt,

Have seen her spirit mount and melt ;

Have joined with her in praise and prayer ;

And cannot, dare not, yet despair.

She that has fed on heavenly food,
Conversed with all that's great and good,
Can she descend from heights like these
To the poor worldling's husks and lees?

She, that has bent at Heaven's high throne,
And claimed its glories for her own,
An earthworm here again to crawl?—
She cannot long so deeply fall.

I know how many for her feel,
And plead with Thee to come and heal:
I know the power of faith and prayer,
And cannot, will not, yet despair.

Sunk as she is in thoughtless sin,
Thou hast a still, small voice within—
A silent hold—a hidden plea—
That needs but quickening, Lord, from Thee.

A look of Thine can life impart ;
A tone of Thine can touch the heart :
The very grave Thy voice must hear :
Oh, bid it reach our sister's ear !

Press on her soul each pang and scorn,
Which Thou for her of old hast borne ;
And ask how she will dare to meet
Thy face upon a Judgment-seat.

Talk to her heart, and bid her feel ;
Send forth Thy word to wound and heal ;
Melt off her spirit's icy chain,
And bid her rise and live again.

She is not dead : Thy voice Divine
Can still revive, and seal her Thine ;
And 'neath Thy wing she yet may dwell,
More meek, more safe, than ere she fell.

The Sailor's Meditation, on Watch at Night

Above me hangs the silent sky ;
　　Around me rolls the sea ;
The crew is all at rest ; and I
　　Am, Lord, alone with Thee !

Go where I may, from all remote,
　　Thou, Lord, art ever near :
No secret thought, but Thou canst note ;
　　No word, but Thou canst hear.

When all around are sunk to sleep,
　　Thy presence here I find :
To me Thou walkest o'er the deep,
　　Or speakest in the wind.

I look up to the starry sky ;
  And read Thy glories there :
I look down to myself, and sigh,
  'Can I be still Thy care ?'

I think of days and dangers past,
  When I have found Thee nigh ;
And wonder how Thy love can last
  To such a worm as I.

I think of terrors yet at hand,
  Of Judgment, and the tomb ;
And ask my soul how it shall stand
  To hear its final doom !

Ah, then, how all I 've been, and done,
  Would fill me with despair,
If to the Cross I could not run,
  And find a Saviour there !

I know He has the power to aid ;
  I know He has the will :
And He, who once for sinners bled,
  Will rescue sinners still.

Lord, arm my soul with faith in Thee,
  And fill my heart with love ;
My path from sin and danger free,
  And guide me safe above.

And while at night the waves I beat,
  Lord, often thus descend,
And grant me here communion sweet
  With Thee, the sailor's Friend.

She is gone! she is gone!

SHE is gone! she is gone! A God of love
Has called her up to His side above :
Has gathered the flower in all its prime,
And bade it bloom in a brighter clime ;
Has filled her hand with a heavenly lyre,
And found her a place in His angel choir.

She is gone! she is gone to a land of light,
Where the glorious day ne'er sinks in night :
Where a cloud ne'er comes across the sky ;
Where the tears are wiped from every eye :
Where all is holiness, love, and bliss,
And none regret such a world as this.

She is gone ! she is gone !   She passed away
Like the dying close of a summer day :
A dawn of glory around her shone,
A light shot down from the Heavenly Throne :
The last of her breath in song was spent,
And forth in a smile her spirit went.

She is gone ! she is gone to her high reward,
To bask in the looks of her wished-for Lord.
She gained one peep through the golden gate ;
She saw the Seraphim for her wait ;
And sprang from sorrow and sin away
To dwell in the light of eternal day.

She is gone! she is gone!   And who would chain
Her soul to a world like ours again ?
But oh, the blank, the desolate void,
In hearts that her converse here enjoyed !
They long from all upon earth to sever,
And be with their loved and lost for ever.

She is gone ! she is gone but a while before,
She waits for them at the heavenly door :
They hear her calling them up on high ;
They feel her drawing them on to the sky ;
And pray, at their parting hour to be
As ripe, as ready, as blessed as she.

Flowers

CHILDREN of dew and sunshine, balmy flowers!
   Ye seem like creatures of a heavenly mould
That linger in this fallen earth of ours,
   Fair relics of her Paradise of old.

Amidst her tombs and ruins, gentle things,
   Ye smile and glitter in celestial bloom ;
Like radiant feathers dropped from angel wings,
   Or tiny rainbows of a world of gloom.

Yes : there is heaven about you : in your breath
   And hues it dwells.   The stars of heaven ye
      shine ;
Bright strangers in a land of sin and death,
   That talk of God, and point to realms divine.

O mutely eloquent ! the heart may read
   In books like you, in tinted leaf or wing,
Fragrance, and music, lessons that exceed
   The formal lore that graver pages bring.

Ye speak of frail humanity : ye tell
   How man, like you, shall flourish and shall fall.
But, ah ! ye speak of Heavenly Love as well,
   And say, the God of flowers is God of all.

While Faith in you her Maker's goodness views
   Beyond her utmost need, her boldest claim,
She catches something of your smiles and hues,
   Forgets her fears, and glows and smiles the
      same.

Childhood and you are playmates; matching well
   Your sunny cheeks, and mingling fragrant
      breath.

Ye help young Love his faltering tale to tell ;
  Ye scatter sweetness o'er the bed of Death.

Sweet flowers, sweet flowers, be mine to dwell
    with you !
  Ye talk of song and sunshine, hope and love :
Ye breathe of all bright things, and lead us
    through
  The best of earth to better still above.

Sweet flowers, sweet flowers! the rich exuberance
  Of Nature's heart in her propitious hours :
When glad emotions in her bosom dance,
  She vents her happiness in laughing flowers.

I love you, when along the fields in spring
  Your dewy eyes look countless from the turf ;
I love you, when from summer boughs you swing,
  As light and silvery as the ocean surf.

I love your earliest beauties, and your last :
    Come when you may, you still are welcome
        here ;
Flinging your sweets on Autumn's dying blast,
    Or weaving chaplets for the infant year.

I love your gentle eyes and smiling faces,
    Bright with the sun, or wet with balmy
        showers ;
Your looks and language in all times and places,
    In lordly gardens, or in woodland bowers.

But most, sweet flowers, I love you, when ye talk
    As Jesus taught you when He o'er you trod ;
And, mingling smiles and morals, bid us walk
    Content o'er earth to glory and to God.

New-Year's Morning Hymn

Hail to another year,
  The year that now begins!
All hail to Him who led us here
  Through dangers and through sins!

Hail to another year!
  Peace to the year that's past!
May this one at its close appear
  Less worthless than the last!

Hail to another year!
  Ere round its wheels are driven,
Each to the grave will stand more near—
  Will each be nearer heaven?

Hail to another year !
Ere half its race is sped,
Ourselves, with all we treasure here,
May rest among the dead.

Hail to another year !
Though yet unknown, untrod,
Whate'er may come, we need not fear,
If friends, through Christ, with God.

Hail to another year,
A year of peace and love !
Oh, may it prove a foretaste here
Of endless years above !

Recollections

'T was a sweet April morning : I traversed the
   glade
Where my light foot in infancy often had played :
Each object recalled to my lingering view
The hours that there once so delightfully flew.

Dear scenes of enchantment, for ever gone by!
How brightly they danced before memory's eye!
I numbered their fugitive blisses all o'er :
They were flown, and I sighed I had prized
   them no more.

Oh, why is it thus, that we never discover
The worth of our joys till possession is over?
That we only can gaze on the sun of delight,
When its fast-fading glories are setting in night?

All aimless and wild as the zephyr, we fleet
O'er a thousand fair flow'rets that smile at our
    feet :
Though they lure us to pluck them, and woo us
    to stay,
We trample, we slight them, and flutter away.

Then, when life brings its crosses, its cares, and
    its fears,
When disaster beside and before us appears,
Then we pause, and look back, and our folly
    discern ;
Then we prize, bless, and mourn what can never
    return.

When all that hope hung on for comfort is flown,
When delights from the past must be gathered
    alone,
How dimly they shine through the distance of
    years !
How ill can they chase present shadows and tears!

Woe, woe to the heart, that is destined to ache
In a world whose gay bustle it loathes to par-
    take !
Where nothing is left that is moving or dear,
That can light up a smile, or elicit a tear!

When conscience is sickened on looking within,
When without there is little to wish or to win,
When Memory shrinks back from the things that
    have been,
And Hope looking onward grows pale at the scene,

Oh, where to find comfort? Oh, whither to fly,
Scarce wishing to live, and yet dreading to die?
Thus helpless, thus reckless, pierced, lost, un-
    forgiven ;
Heart-broken on earth, and desponding of
    heaven !

Lord, Thou canst give light in this hour of de-
    spair ;
Canst ease us of anguish, or teach us to bear :

And good is the pressure of pain and distress,
If they lead to a Saviour to heal and to bless.

'T is good that our props should from 'neath us
    be fled,
If we drop into Arms Everlasting instead;
That thistles and thorns in our pathway should
    rise,
If they send us but on for repose to the skies.

When all else is changing within and around,
In God and His goodness no change can be
    found.
In giving or taking His end is the same,
His creatures to quicken, exalt, and reclaim.

Such terrors to drive, and such love to allure,
Lord, add but Thy grace, and the issue is sure.
My trials may thicken, my comforts may flee;
I 'm rich amid ruin with heaven and Thee.

The World renounced

Go, worthless world!   I've tried and found
   Thy hollowness at last :
I know thee now an empty sound,
   And spurn at all thou hast.

Thy smiles, thy flatteries, thy deceit,
   I 've scanned them o'er and o'er.
Go, other hearts to snare and cheat ;
   Thou holdest mine no more.

I 've been thy dupe, I 've been thy scoff,
   For years I 've worn thy chain :
My Saviour came and called me off,
   And I am free again :

Free with the freedom Christ bestows ;
   Divinely, greatly free ;
Redeemed from follies, sins, and woes ;
   Redeemed, false world, from thee !

Still must I linger 'mid thy slaves,
   A stranger yet a while ;
Must toss on thy uncertain waves,
   And meet thy specious smile :

The scoffs of pride, the snares of sense,
   Must still my firmness try ;
Till Christ returns to call me hence
   To peace with Him on high.

I know me weak, and prone to fall ;
   Yet know, with Him my friend,
I still may pass unhurt through all
   To glory in the end.

And while my sojourn here I make,
This, this my maxim be,—
To love mankind for Jesus' sake,
And spurn, false world, at thee.

'Is this thy Kindness to thy Friend?'

ALTERED FROM QUARLES

Oh, think, how He, whom thou hast wounded,
   Hast scourged, and scorned, and spit upon,
Hath paid thy ransom, and compounded
   For thy distresses with His own !
How He, whose blood thy sins have spilt,
   Whose limbs they to the Cross have nailed,
Hath freely borne thy load of guilt,
   And made supply where thou hast failed.

He died, to save thy soul from dying ;
   Was bound Himself, to set thee free ;
And where there was no power of flying,
   He came, and met the blow for thee ;

And all this dying friend requires,
    For all His pity, all His pain,
Are simple aims, and pure desires,
    And for His love like love again.

Oh, loose then, Lord, my tardy tears,
    And break this fleshly rock asunder,
And on my night of doubts and fears
    Pour a new day of joy and wonder.
This deadness from my soul remove ;
    Melt down my icy unbelief ;
Let grief add feeling to my love,
    And love pluck out the sting from grief.

Then rise, poor earthworm, from the dust ;
    Enjoy thy new and large condition ;
Walk with thy God in humble trust,
    And ripen for His full fruition.

No more rebellious, dark, exiled,
    Adore, and love, and praise Him rather ;
Return a lost, but contrite, child,
    And find a kind, forgiving Father.

The Infant's Address to departing Day-light

BEAUTIFUL Day-light, stay, oh, stay,
Nor fly from the world and me away,
To darken the skies, so blue and bright,
And take the green fields from my lonely sight.
No birds then will talk to me from the tall tree,
Nor flowers appear looking and laughing on me.
Kind voices I hear, and kind faces I view;
But I can't talk with them, little birds, as with
    you :
I know not their language, their ways, and their
    looks,
Nor care for their candles, pens, pencils, and
    books.
Then, beautiful Day-light, fly not yet !
Few suns have I ever seen rise or set ;

And when each day with its pleasures is o'er,

I fear they will never come back any more.

A stranger I am in this world below,

And have much of its wonders to mark and know:

I want to see more of each new fairy scene,

To trace sounds and objects, and learn what

    they mean ;

To gaze on the features of her in whose breast

I am fed, and folded, and sung into rest,

Who kisses me softly, and calls me her dear,

And all the new friends that are kind to me here.

Then stay, sweet Day-light, mine eyes to bless !

I know Night little, and love it still less.

The place that I came from had nothing of shade,

In beauty and glory for ever arrayed :

There angel forms were smiling and singing,

And waving their wings in the Day-light springing

From God's own face, like a fountain flowing

With rays sun and moon must fail in bestowing.

I scarcely remember that land of bliss ;

But I love what is brightest and purest in this :

And if upon one of those clouds I could lie,

That have run to the verge of the western sky,

And there, in rosy companionship seated,

Look down on the sun from earth retreated ;

If aloft in its bright fleecy folds I could lay me,

And call on the winds through the skies to
    convey me,

I 'd ride round the world the perennial attendant

On Day-light, wherever it shone most resplendent;

Over hills, over fogs, I would take my glad flight,

And bathe and revel in rivers of light.

The moon and the stars I would leave behind ;

Nor stoop any object on earth to mind ;

Unless for her baby dear mother should cry :

Then I 'd glide down to tell her how happy was I ;

I 'd kiss off her tears, and wish her good day,

And again on my travels away, away !

Sweet bird, thy suit it is vain to press,

The Day-light heeds not thy fond address;

On glittering pinion away he hies,

To meet other wishes, and light other skies:

The will of his God he goes to obey,

Nor at earthly bidding will haste or stay.

A child of light, sweet bird, thou art now,

Nor needest a veil for thy conscious brow:

No deeds thy tiny hands have done

Need fear the broad eye of the flaring sun;

And the pleasant and pure of this world of woe,

Is all thy delicate spirit can know.

But ah, my baby! the day may appear

When the light shall be loathed as it now is dear;

When thy red-rolling eye, that can weep no
    more,

The relief of night shall in vain implore!

The billows and storms of a heart-breaking world

O'er each young illusion too soon may be hurled;

May wring thee, may wreck thee, till all is riven,

But the friendship of God and the refuge of heaven.

Yet baby, my baby, if these shall be thine,

Thou 'lt not want a spot where thy head may
    recline ;

Thou 'lt not want a light in this world of dismay

To guide thee from danger, or solace thy way :

The bright Sun of Righteousness never declines,

The light of the Gospel eternally shines ;

Adds zest to our joys, plucks the sting from
    our woes,

Lends peace to our life, and joy to its close.

This light, my boy, be it thine to prize !

It ne'er will withdraw from thy favoured eyes :

Come joy, or come sorrow, the same it will stay,

And shine more and more to the perfect day ;

Till grace is glory, and faith is sight,

And God, as at first, 'mid His sons of light,

Receives His homage of song and love,

And thou art with Him for ever above.

'It is I: be not afraid'

Loud was the wind, and wild the tide ;
  The ship her course delayed :
The Lord came to their help, and cried,
  ''T is I : be not afraid.'

Who walks the waves in wondrous guise,
  By Nature's laws unstayed ?
''T is I,' a well-known voice replies ;
  ''T is I : be not afraid.'

He mounts the deck : down lulls the sea ;
  The tempest is allayed ;
The prostrate crew adore ; and He
  Exclaims, ' Be not afraid.'

Thus, when the storm of life is high,
    Come, Saviour, to my aid !
Come, when no other help is nigh,
    And say, ' Be not afraid.'

Speak, and my griefs no more are heard ;
    Speak, and my fears are laid ;
Speak, and my soul shall bless the word,
    '"T is I : be not afraid.'

When on the bed of death I lie,
    And stretch my hands for aid,
Stand Thou before my glazing eye,
    And say, ' Be not afraid.'

Before Thy judgment-seat above
    When nature sinks dismayed,
Oh, cheer me with a word of love—
    '"T is I : be not afraid.'

Worlds may around to wreck be driven,
    If then I hear it said,
By Him who rules through earth and heaven,
    '"T is I : be not afraid.'

Inscription on a Monument

TO S— P— S—

WHAT shall we write on this memorial stone?

Thy merits?   Thou didst rest on Christ's alone.

Our sorrows?   Thou wouldst chide the selfish
    tear.

Our love?   Alas, it needs no record here.

Praise to thy God and ours?   His truth and
    love

Are sung in nobler strains by thee above.

What wouldst thou have us write?—A voice is
    heard,—

' Write, for each reader write, a warning word.

' Bid him look well before him, and within ;

' Talk to his heedless heart of death and sin ;

' And if at these he tremble, bid him flee

' To Christ, and find Him all in all, like me.'

The Prayer-answering God

I STAND in a world where there's nothing my
own,
  Where the lightest event is beyond my con-
    trol;
But to Him that is Ruler supreme and alone
  I gladly resign, for I know Him, the whole.
How pleasant, 'mid changes and chances un-
    thought,
  On His wisdom and love to disburthen our
    care;
And to know, that the God who disposes our
    lot
  Is a God that will hear and will answer our
    prayer!

There are those that I love, far away from me
now,
  And roaming through danger by shore and
by sea ;
And what were my feelings, my Father, if
Thou
  Wert less than Almighty for them and for
me?
I cannot command the wild winds to be still ;
  I cannot compel the dark waves to forbear ;
But One is above them who can, and who will :
  In Him I am strong, for he answereth prayer.

Ah me! I gaze round me,—and what are the
smiles
  And the looks that give life all its zest and
its soul?
Mortality claims them, and sternly reviles
  Affection's vain struggle against her control.

I own it, I feel it ; yet, humbled and awed,
  I still dare to love them, all frail as they are ;
For I know we are both in the hands of our
    God,
  The Father of Jesus, the Hearer of prayer.

Then here be my resting-place ! here will I sit
  Secure 'mid the shiftings of time and event ;
For Fate has no power but what He may permit,
  And the Hand that must take is the same that
    hath lent.
On His wisdom and goodness I calmly rely ;
  Whate'er He assigns He can aid me to bear :
He knows what is good for me better than I,
  And will give it, I hope, in despite of my
    prayer.

The Heart in tune

Be the heart in tune within,
  All without runs smooth and even,
And earth's objects seem to win
  Something of the hues of heaven :
Clouds from off our sky are flown ;
  All grows bright around and o'er us ;
Life acquires a loftier tone,
  And hope dances light before us :

Music comes in every gale ;
  Flowers in all our paths are blowing ;
Prosperous winds fill every sail ;
  Tides are ever fair and flowing :

Time adds feathers to his wing ;
   Grief of half his load is lightened ;
Life's distresses lose their sting,
   And its every joy is heightened.

Then the waste, where 'er we roam,
   Gushes with refreshing fountains ;
Then between us and our home
   Ope the seas, and sink the mountains :
Faith is strong, and views are clear ;
   Foes or fears no more confound us ;
Ministering angels near,
   And an Eden opening round us :

Nature through her wide domain
   Quits her air of ruined sadness,
Kindles into smiles again,
   Wakes anew to song and gladness :

God amid His works appears,
   Calls His creatures to adore Him;
And this world of sin and tears
   Blossoms as the rose before Him.

If His gospel then be heard,
   Soon the inmost soul it reaches;
God speaks home in every word,
   Christ again in person teaches;
Every promise is applied,
   Power to every precept given,
And the Spirit and the Bride
   Point and woo us on to heaven.

Prayer and praise are easy then,
   From the soul spontaneous flowing;
And with love to God and men
   Tenderly the heart is glowing.

All our duties lighter grow ;
  Pleasant seems the meanest station ;
And from light to light we go
  To the fulness of salvation.

Be our spirits ever such,
  Tuned into harmonious meetness,
Till their chords to every touch
  Answer in some tone of sweetness ;
Quickened by celestial grace,
  Purified of earthly leaven,
Shining, like the Prophet's face,
  With a glory caught from heaven.

Domestic Love

EXTRACT FROM AN UNPUBLISHED POEM

How lovely is domestic harmony,
Where mind on mind and heart on heart repose
Undoubting; and the friends, whom Providence
Has cast together, sharing each with each
Their hopes, their joys, their cares, appear to live
One common life, and breathe one common will!
This fallen world brings forth no other flower
So beautiful as this; and where the love
Of God is added to this love of man,
Somewhat of heaven itself to earth descends.
For what is heaven, but one immortal home,
Where all are brother, Parent, child, or friend,

And all are happy, loving and beloved?

And what is hell, but the abode of hate

And envy, where discordant elements

Mingle, and hiss, and jar eternally?

Bright comes the morn and soft descends the
    night

On the fair dwelling-place of love and peace :

And from the buffetings of this rude world

Its happy inmates, like the wandering dove

Home to her ark, for refuge there can fly.

Prayer meets no hindrance there ; and praise '
    from thence,

Of hearts and lips in unison, ascends

More acceptable to the God of love.

The idol Self is from his throne cast down,

And God set up instead ; and where He reigns

There must be happiness, there must be heaven.

Sad Thoughts

1815

Yes, I am calm, am humbled now ;
   The storm is rocked to rest ;
And I have learnt my head to bow,
   And count my lot the best.

I would not struggle with my God,
   Or chide what He has given :
Why should I murmur at the rod
   That drives me on to heaven ?

Yet withering thoughts at times will break
   Across my calmer frame ;
And then I feel how hearts may ache,
   Though still they bow the same.

Dark moods, too long and fondly nursed,
   Will o'er me come unsought :
And thou, ah thou, beloved the first,
   To be the last forgot !

I meet thy pensive, moonlight face ;
   Thy thrilling voice I hear ;
And former hours and scenes retrace,
   Too fleeting, and too dear !

Then sighs and tears flow fast and free,
   Though none is nigh to share ;
And life has nought beside for me
   So sweet as this despair.

There are crushed hearts that will not break ;
   And mine, methinks, is one ;
Or thus I should not weep and wake,
   And thou to slumber gone.

I little thought it thus could be
  In days more sad and fair—
That earth could have a place for me,
  And thou no longer there.

We met in childhood's morning road;
  Our love with life began;
And on through years the current flowed,
  And deepened as it ran.

Yes: on we loved, and loved the same,
  Though little either said:
It burned, that sad and secret flame,
  Like lamps among the dead.

I knew her heart was all my own;
  She knew the same of mine;
Though caution guarded every tone,
  And checked each outward sign.

To selves or others unexpressed,
  The truth within us waked—
A conscious wound in either breast,
  That inly bled and ached.

At last it came, the day to part!
  And feelings, long repressed,
In bitter shrift from heart to heart
  Were all at length expressed.

That trying hour all barriers broke;
  A frenzy o'er me fell:
Spirit to spirit briefly spoke,
  And then—Farewell! Farewell!

From that dark day I walked alone
  In this wide world of care,
My widowed heart regardless grown
  Of aught that wooed it there.

Its joys and griefs I learned to view
   Without a smile or sigh ;
And nought seemed left me now to do,
   But lay me down and die.

Bereavement was not long her dower ;
   She feels no more its sway :
She pined, she drooped, my severed flower !
   And passed from earth away.

No plaint she breathed, no pain confessed,
   But calmly fell asleep ;
She stole into her grave for rest,
   And left me here to weep.

While thou wert here, there was a hope,
   All dimly as it shone :
'T is gone ! and I am left to cope
   With this cold world alone.

Yet death cannot our hearts divide,
    Or make thee less my own.
'T were sweeter sleeping at thy side
    Than watching here alone.

Yet never, never can we part,
    While Memory holds her reign :
Thine, thine is still this withered heart,
    Till we shall meet again.

That meet we shall, I do not fear :
    The thought was joy to thee :
And I have now but little here
    To part my God and me.

I feel, too, in my darkest mood,
    How much my soul has won :
I know 't was needful all, and good ;
    And say, ' Thy will be done ! '

Still, thoughts like these at times will come,
My firmness to surprise.
When shall I be with thee at home,
Beyond the reach of sighs?

Pleading for Mercy

When at Thy footstool, Lord, I bend,
  And plead with Thee for mercy there,
O think Thou of the sinner's Friend,
  And for His sake receive my prayer !
O think not of my shame and guilt,
  My thousand stains of deepest dye :
Think of the blood which Jesus spilt,
  And let that blood my pardon buy.

Think, Lord, how I am still Thy own,
  The trembling creature of Thy hand ;
Think how my heart to sin is prone,
  And what temptations round me stand.

O think how blind and weak am I,
How strong and wily are my foes :
They wrestled with Thy hosts on high ;
How should a worm their might oppose !

O think upon Thy holy word,
And every plighted promise there—
How prayer should evermore be heard,
And how Thy glory is to spare.
O think not of my doubts and fears,
My strivings with Thy grace divine :
Think upon Jesus' woes and tears,
And let His merits stand for mine.

Thine eye, Thine ear, they are not dull ;
Thine arm can never shortened be :
Behold me here—my heart is full—
Behold, and spare and succour me.

No claim, no merits, Lord, I plead ;
I come a humbled helpless slave :
But, ah ! the more my guilty need,
The more Thy glory, Lord, to save.

To Ellen

WEEPING IN CHURCH ON THE ANNIVERSARY OF
HER FATHER'S DEATH, WHEN FIFTEEN
YEARS OLD.

Ah! wherefore should the silent tear
  Down Ellen's youthful visage stray,
When such a Hand unseen is near
  To wipe each falling drop away ;
A hand that bears a balm from high,
For every earthly tear and sigh ?

And wherefore mourn a parent's doom,
  When such a Parent from above
Extends His arms and bids her come,
  And dwell with Him whose name is Love ;
Who ne'er that orphan will disown,
Whom Jesus' blood has made His own ?

That gentle Hand, ah! would she see
  And prove its power to soothe and heal!
Ah! would she to that Father flee,
  And know how well He loves her weal!
Ah! would she learn how sweet it is
Through Christ to be for ever His!—

Come, then, and give that heart to Him,
  Which long has dwelt on meaner things :
Come, find thy song a worthier theme,
  And learn to soar on loftier wings.
He who has died that thou mightst live.
Deserves the best 't is thine to give.

The Spirit seeks to live thy Friend,
  And Christ thy brother deigns to be ;
The joys, that know nor bounds nor end,
  To thy possession all are free.
Whate'er is lovely, pure, or great,
On Ellen now vouchsafes to wait.

Expectant angels cry, ' O come !'
  And saints prepare their gladdest song,
Those wandering feet to welcome home,
  Which fifteen years have strayed too long :
Come, then, and all shall triumph o'er
One dear, lost, rescued sinner more.

On Dreaming of my Mother

Stay, gentle shadow of my mother, stay:
Thy form but seldom comes to bless my sleep.
Ye faithless slumbers, flit not thus away,
And leave my wistful eyes to wake and weep.
Oh! I was dreaming of those golden days
When, will my guide, and pleasure all my aim,
I rambled wild through childhood's flowery maze,
And knew of sorrow scarcely by her name.
Those scenes are fled! and thou, alas, art fled,
Light of my heart, and guardian of my youth!
Then come no more to slumbering fancy's bed,
To aggravate the pangs of waking truth:
Or, if kind sleep these visions will restore,
Oh, let me sleep again, and never waken more!

'It doth not yet appear what we shall be'

YE lingering hours, wheel swift away,
And usher in the joyful day,
When, rising from a world like this,
My soul shall dwell where Jesus is!

Too long I 've waited here below,
And spread my wings, and sighed to go!
Too long I 've cried, Blest Saviour, come,
And bear me to Thyself and home!

How favoured they, who once on earth
Enjoyed Thy converse, felt Thy worth;
Who had Thee for their friend and guest,
And leaned their heads upon Thy breast!

How blest, to look up in Thy face,
And there Thy Father's image trace !
To hear the music of Thy tongue,
And learn from thence how angels sung !

A lot like this is not for me,
On earth to thus converse with Thee ;
And tell what I have seen, and heard,
And handled, of the Incarnate Word.

Yet do I hope at last to rise,
And join my Lord above the skies ;
Close by His feet to take my place,
And see and praise Him face to face ;

To view Him 'mid His flock, and share
With them the mighty Shepherd's care ;
To hear His saints their tributes pay,
And be myself as loud as they.

Till time shall bring this glad event,
I linger here in banishment;
And but for what I taste of Him,
My lot were yet more blank and dim.

But through the gloom at times He looks,
My hopes revives, my fears rebukes,
And bids me here a foretaste prove
Of all I seek with Him above.

Then haste, ye lingering hours, away,
And bring the full unclouded day,
That bears me from a world like this,
And lands me safe where Jesus is!

‘ O that I had wings like a dove, for then

would I fly away and be at rest ’

Oh, had I, my Saviour, the wings of a dove,
How soon would I soar to Thy presence above!
How soon would I flee where the weary have rest,
And hide all my cares in Thy sheltering breast.

I flutter, I struggle, and long to be free ;
I feel me a captive while banished from Thee.
A pilgrim and stranger the desert I roam ;
And look on to Heaven, and fain would be home.

Ah, there the wild tempest for ever shall cease ;
No billow shall ruffle that haven of peace.
Temptation and trouble alike shall depart,
All tears from the eye, and all sin from the heart.

Soon, soon may this Eden of promise be mine!
Rise, bright sun of glory, no more to decline!
Thy light, yet unrisen, the wilderness cheers,
Oh, what will it be, when the fulness appears!

Friends lost in 1833

Gone?—Have ye all then gone,—
The good, the beautiful, the kind, the dear?
Passed to your glorious rest so swiftly on,
And left me weeping here?

I gaze on your bright track;
I hear your lessening voices as ye go.
Have ye no sign, no solace, to fling back
To us who toil below?

They hear not my faint cry;
Beyond the range of sense for ever flown,
I see them melt into eternity,
And feel I am alone.

Into the haven pass'd,
They anchor far beyond the scathe of ill;
While the stern billow, and the reckless blast
    Are mine to cope with still.

Oh! from that land of love,
Look ye not sometimes on this world of woe?
Think you not, dear ones, in bright bowers
        above,
    Of those you 've left below?

Surely ye note us here,
Though not as we appear to mortal view;
And can we still, with all our stains, be dear
    To spirits pure as you?

Do ye not loathe,—not spurn,—
The worms of clay, the slaves of sense and will?
When ye from God and glory earthward turn,
    Oh! can ye love us still?

Or, have ye rather now
Drunk of His Spirit whom ye worship there,
Who stripp'd the crown of glory from His brow,
   The platted thorns to wear?

Is it a fair fond thought,
That you may still our friends and guardians be,
And Heaven's high ministry by you be wrought
   With abjects low as we?

May we not sweetly hope
That you around our path and bed may dwell?
And shall not all our blessings brighter drop
   From hands we loved so well?

Shall we not feel you near
In hours of danger, solitude, and pain,
Cheering the darkness, drying off the tear,
   And turning loss to gain?

Shall not your gentle voice
Break on temptation's dark and sullen mood,
Subdue our erring will, o'errule our choice,
        And win from ill to good?

        O yes! to us, to us
A portion of your converse still be given:
Struggling affection still would hold you thus,
        Nor yield you all to Heaven!

    Lead our faint steps to God;
Be with us while the desert here we roam;
Teach us to tread the path which you have trod,
        To find with you our home!

Stanzas to J. K.

WHAT strains are these, what sweet familiar
     numbers,
  From old Ierne o'er the waters wend?
How welcome, wakening from its lengthen'd
     slumbers,
  Sounds the heart-music of my earliest Friend!
Well might that hand amid the chords have
     falter'd,
  That voice have lost the power to melt and
     move :
How pleasant, then, to find them still unalter'd,
  That lyre in sweetness, and that heart in love!

Shall not my tuneful powers, too long neglected,
  Revive to answer that persuasive call?—
Like the old harp that, mould'ring and rejected,
  Hangs up in silence in some lonely hall,

When youth and beauty's train there re-assembles,
 And mirth and song once more begin to flow,
Light o'er the chords a mimic music trembles,
 Responsive to the notes that swell below !

Ah me !—what thoughts those few bold notes
     awaken,—
 Bright recollections of life's morning hours ;
Haunts long remembered, and too soon forsaken ;
   Days that fled by in sunshine, song, and
     flowers ;
Old Clogher's rocks, our own sequester'd valley ;
   Wild walks by moonlight on the sounding
     shore,
Hearts warm and free, light laugh, and playful
     sally,
 All that has been,—and shall return no more—

No more,—no more,—moods ever new and
     changing,
 Feelings that forth in song so freely gush'd,

Wing'd hopes, high fancies, thoughts unfetter'd
  ranging—
  Flowers which the world's cold ploughshare
  since has crush'd.
Dear early visions of departed gladness,
  Ye rise, ye live a moment in that strain,
A gleam of sunshine on life's wintry sadness,
  Ah! why so bright, to flit so soon again?

Friend of my heart!—since those young visions
  perish'd,
  We 've trod a chequer'd path of good and ill;
We 've seen the wreck of much that once we
  cherish'd,
  But not the wreck of love and friendship still.
No, hand in hand we 've met life's stormy weather,
  Sustain'd the buffetings of foe and friend,
And hand in hand and heart in heart together,
  We 'll help and cheer each other to the end.

Strike then the chords!—alas, too rarely stricken,

  And I will answer in my humbler style :

No voice like thine can soothe, can urge, can

    quicken,—

  Why has it been so little heard ere while ?

Yes, strike the chords ! high thoughts and aims

    inspiring ;

  And up the narrow way we'll homeward move,

Mingling our pilgrim songs, and here acquiring

  New hearts and voices for the songs above.

BERRYHEAD, 1840.

Sea Changes

FROM shore to shore the waters sleep,
　Without a breath to move them ;
And mirror many a fathom deep
　Rocks round, and skies above them.
I catch the sea-bird's lightest wail
　That dots the distant billow,
And hear the flappings of the sail
　That lull the sea-boy's pillow.

Anon—across the glassy bay
　The catspaw gusts come creeping :
A thousand waves are soon at play,
　In sunny freshness leaping.

The surge once more talks round the shore,
　The good ship walks the ocean ;
Seas, skies, and men all wake again
　To music, health, and motion.

But now the clouds, in angry crowds,
　On Heaven's grim forehead muster,
And wild and wide sweeps o'er the tide
　The white squall's fitful bluster.
The stout ship heels, the brave heart reels
　Before the 'whelming breaker ;
And all in nature quakes, and feels
　The presence of its Maker.

Oh, glorious still in every form,
　Untamed, untrodden ocean ;
Beneath the sunshine, or the storm,
　In stillness, or commotion ;

Be mine to dwell beside the swell,

A witness of thy wonders;

Feel thy light spray around me play,

And thrill before thy thunders!

While yet a boy I felt it joy

To gaze upon thy glories;

I loved to ride thy stormy tide,

And shout in joyous chorus.

With calmer brow I haunt thee now,

To nurse sublime emotion;

My soul is awed and filled with God,

By thee, majestic ocean!

1840.

David's three Mighty Ones

'And David longed, and said, Oh that one would give me drink of the water of the well of Bethlehem, which is by the gate!'—2 SAM. xxiii. 15

FAINT on Rephaim's sultry side
   Sat Israel's warrior-king ;
'Oh for one draught,' the hero cried,
   'From Bethlehem's cooling spring !—
From Bethlehem's spring, upon whose brink
My youthful knee bent down to drink !

'I know the spot, by yonder gate,
   Beside my father's home,
Where pilgrims love at eve to wait,
   And girls for water come.
Oh for that healing water now,
To quench my lip, to cool my brow !

'But round that gate, and in that home,
  And by that sacred well,
Now hostile feet insulting roam,
  And impious voices swell.
The Philistine holds Bethlehem's halls,
While we pine here beneath its walls.'—

Three gallant men stood nigh, and heard
  The wish their king expressed;
Exchanged a glance, but not a word,
  And dash'd from 'midst the rest.
And strong in zeal, with ardour flushed,
They up the hill to Bethlehem rushed.

The foe fast mustering to attack,
  Their fierceness could not rein;
No friendly voice could call them back.—
  'Shall David long in vain?
Long for a cup from Bethlehem's spring,
And none attempt the boon to bring?'

And now the city gate they gain,
  And now in conflict close;
Unequal odds! three dauntless men
  Against unnumbered foes.
Yet through their ranks they plough their way
Like galleys through the ocean spray.

The gate is forced, the crowd is pass'd;
  They scour the open street;
While hosts are gathering fierce and fast
  To block up their retreat.
Haste back! haste back, ye desperate Three!
Or Bethlehem soon your grave must be!

They come again;—and with them bring—
  Nor gems nor golden prey;
A single cup from Bethlehem's spring
  Is all they bear away;
And through the densest of the train
Fight back their glorious way again.

O'er broken shields and prostrate foes
   They urge their conquering course.
Go, try the tempest to oppose,
   Arrest the lightning's force ;
But hope not, Pagans, to withstand
The shock of Israel's chosen band !

Hurrah ! hurrah ! again they're free ;
   And 'neath the open sky,
On the green turf they bend the knee,
   And lift the prize on high ;
Then onward through the shouting throng
To David bear their spoil along.

All in their blood and dust they sink
   Full low before their king.
' Again,' they cry, ' let David drink
   Of his own silver spring ;
And if the draught our lord delight,
His servants' toil 't will well requite.'

With deep emotion David took
From their red hands the cup ;
Cast on its stains a shuddering look,
And held it heavenward up.
' I prize your boon,' exclaimed the king,
' But dare not taste the draught you bring.

' I prize the zeal that perill'd life,
A wish of mine to crown ;
I prize the might that in the strife
Bore foes by thousands down :—
But dare not please myself with aught
By Israel's blood and peril bought.

' To Heaven the glorious spoil is due ;
And His the offering be,
Whose arm has borne you safely through,
My brave, but reckless, Three !'—
Then on the earth the cup he pour'd,
A free libation to the Lord.

There is a well in Bethlehem still,
  A fountain, at whose brink
The weary soul may rest at will,
  The thirsty stoop and drink :
And unrepelled by foe or fence
Draw living waters freely thence.

Oh, did we thirst, as David then,
  For this diviner spring !
Had we the zeal of David's men
  To please a Higher King !
What precious draughts we thence might drain,
What holy triumphs daily gain !

A Recall to my Child A. M.

JUNE 1, 1839

Come back, come back, my blessed child !
    Come home, my own light-hearted !
Papa, they say, has rarely smiled
    Since from his side you parted.—
That face which beams like opening day,
    That laugh which never wearies ;
Why do they linger still away ?
    Come home, dear girl, and cheer us !

I saunter sadly through my hours,—
    They want one voice to mend them ;
A spell is o'er my drooping flowers,—
    They pine for you to tend them.

'The fairest now look all amiss,
   Too dingy, or too flaunting.—
And are they changed? ah, no, 't is this—
   The sweetest flower is wanting !

Young spring at last, despite the shocks
   Of winter's lingering bluster,
Has flung her mantle o'er our rocks,
   And clothed our hills with lustre.
Music, and balm, and beauty play
   In all around and o'er us.
' Come, truant, come,' all seem to say .
   ' Come, join our happy chorus.'

' Come,' cries the cowslip's fading bell ;
   ' Come,' cries the ripening cherry ;
' Come, ere the bloom in every dell
   Is turn'd to pod and berry ;

Come, ere the cuckoo change his tone ;
  Ere from her nest the linnet,
With all her little ones, is flown,
  And you 've ne'er peep'd within it.'

The sun sets not so brightly now,
  Across the golden water,
As when it gleam'd upon the brow
  Of my loved absent daughter.
Home has no more its cheerful tone,
  Its healthful hue about it :—
When from the lyre one chord is gone
  The rest sound ill without it.

Come back ; the city's flaunting crowd,
  The concert's formal measures,
The din of fashion, false and loud,
  Are not like nature's pleasures.—

These, these alone, the heart can touch,
　　Are simplest and sincerest.
You have an eye, a soul for such :
　　Come home, and share them, dearest.

Come, at my side, again to walk
　　Beside the fresh'ning billow.
Come, where the waves all night will talk
　　To you upon your pillow.
Come, where the skiff on sunny seas
　　For you is lightly riding ;
Where health and song in every breeze
　　My absent girl come chiding.

Come back ! we all from your glad eyes
　　New light and life will borrow.
'T is not papa alone that sighs,
　　' Why leave me to my sorrow ?'

Each, all, in your loved converse miss
  Some wonted source of pleasure,
From look, or tone, or smile, or kiss :
  Come home, come home, my treasure !

Declining Days

'Quodsi vita est optanda sapienti, profecto nullam aliam ob causam vivere optaverim, quam ut aliquid efficiam, quod vita dignum sit: et quod utilitatem legentibus, etsi non ad eloquentiam, quia tenuis in nobis eloquentiæ rivus est, ad vivendum tamen adferat: quod est maxime necessarium. Quo profecto, satis me vixisse arbitrabor, et officium hominis implesse, si labor meus aliquos homines ab erroribus liberatos, ad iter cæleste direxerit.'—
LACTANTIUS, De Opif. Dei, cap. xx.

WHY do I sigh to find
Life's evening shadows gathering round my way?
The keen eye dimming, and the buoyant mind
    Unhinging day by day?

    Is it the natural dread
Of that stern lot, which all who live must see?
The worm, the clay, the dark and narrow bed,—
    Have these such awe for me?

Can I not summon pride
To fold my decent mantle round my breast;
And lay me down at nature's Eventide,
Calm to my dreamless rest?

As nears my soul the verge
Of this dim continent of woe and crime,
Shrinks she to hear Eternity's long surge
Break on the shores of Time?

Asks she, how she shall fare
When conscience stands before the Judge's
throne,
And gives her record in, and all shall there
Know, as they all are known?

A solemn scene and time—
And well may Nature quail to feel them near—
But grace in feeble breasts can work sublime,
And faith o'ermaster fear!

Hark ! from that throne comes down
A voice which strength to sinking souls can give,
That voice all Judgment's thunders cannot drown ;
    ' Believe,' it cries, ' and live.'

Weak—sinful, as I am,
That still small voice forbids me to despond ;
Faith clings for refuge to the bleeding Lamb,
    Nor dreads the gloom beyond.—

'T is not, then, earth's delights
From which my spirit feels so loath to part :
Nor the dim future's solemn sounds or sights
    That press so on my heart.

No ! 't is the thought that I—
My lamp so low, my sun so nearly set,
Have lived so useless, so unmissed should die :—
    'T is this, I now regret.—

I would not be the wave
That swells and ripples up to yonder shore ;
That drives impulsive on, the wild wind's slave,
And breaks, and is no more !—

I would not be the breeze,
That murmurs by me in its viewless play,
Bends the light grass, and flutters in the trees,
And sighs and flits away !

No ! not like wave or wind
Be my career across the earthly scene ;
To come and go, and leave no trace behind
To say that I have been.

I want not vulgar fame —
I seek not to survive in brass or stone ;
Hearts may not kindle when they hear my name,
Nor tears my value own.—

But might I leave behind
Some blessing for my fellows, some fair trust
To guide, to cheer, to elevate my kind
When I was in the dust.

Within my narrow bed
Might I not wholly mute or useless be ;
But hope that they, who trampled o'er my head,
Drew still some good from me !

Might my poor lyre but give
Some simple strain, some spirit-moving lay ;
Some sparklet of the Soul, that still might live
When I was passed to clay !—

Might verse of mine inspire
One virtuous aim, one high resolve impart ;
Light in one drooping soul a hallow'd fire,
Or bind one broken heart.—

Death would be sweeter then,
More calm my slumber 'neath the silent sod ;
Might I thus live to bless my fellow-men,
Or glorify my God !

Why do we ever lose,
As judgment ripens, our diviner powers ?
Why do we only learn our gifts to use
When they no more are ours ?

O Thou ! whose touch can lend
Life to the dead, Thy quick'ning grace supply,
And grant me, swanlike, my last breath to spend
In song that may not die !

The Dying Christian to his Soul

Bird of my breast, away!
The long-wish'd hour is come!
On to the realms of cloudless day,
On to thy glorious home!

Long has been thine to mourn
In banishment and pain.
Return, thou wand'ring dove, return,
And find thy ark again!

Away, on joyous wing,
Immensity to range;
Around the throne to soar and sing,
And faith for sight exchange.

Lo ! to the golden gate
What shining thousands come !
My trembling Soul, for thee they wait,
To guard and guide thee home.

Hark ! from on high they speak,
That bright and blessed train,
' Rise, Heaven-born spirit, rise, and seek
Thy rest in Heavenly gain.

' Sweet are the songs above,
Where hearts are all in tune ;
They feed upon unfailing love,
And bask in glory's noon.

' Their struggles all are still,
Their days of darkness o'er ;
At rapture's fount they drink at will,
And drink for evermore.

' Flee, then, from sin and woe ;
   To joys immortal flee ;
Quit thy dark prison-house below,
   And be for ever free !'

   I come, ye blessed throng,
   Your tasks and joys to share ;
Oh, fill my lips with holy song,
   My drooping wing upbear.

   Friends of my heart, adieu !
   I cannot weep to-day ;
The tears that nature prompts for you
   Are dried in glory's ray.

   I see the King of kings,
   His glorious voice I hear.
Oh, who can dwell on earthly things
   With Heaven so bright and near ?

Napoleon's Grave

ADDRESSED TO THE FRENCH NATION ON THEIR PRO-
POSING TO REMOVE NAPOLEON'S REMAINS
FROM ST. HELENA TO FRANCE

DISTURB him not! he slumbers well
    On his rock 'mid the western deep,
Where the broad blue waters round him swell,
    And the tempests o'er him sweep.
Oh, leave him where his mountain bed
    Looks o'er the Atlantic wave,
And the mariner high in the far grey sky
    Points out Napoleon's grave!

There, 'midst three mighty continents
    That trembled at his word,
Wrapt in his shroud of airy cloud,
    Sleeps Europe's warrior lord:

And there, on the heights, still seems to stand,
  At eve, his shadowy form ;
His grey capote on the mist to float,
  And his voice in the midnight storm.

Disturb him not ! though bleak and bare,
  That spot is all his own ;
And truer homage was paid him there
  Than on his hard-won throne.
Earth's trembling monarchs there at bay
  The cagèd lion kept ;
For they knew with dread that his iron tread
  Woke earthquakes where he stept.

Disturb him not ! vain France, thy clime
  No resting-place supplies,
So meet, so glorious, so sublime,
  As that where thy Hero lies.

Mock not that grim and mouldering wreck !
  Revere that bleaching brow !
Nor call the dead from his grave to deck
  A puppet pageant now !

Born in a time when blood and crime
  Raged through thy realm at will,
He waved his hand o'er the troubled land,
  And the storm at once was still.
He reared from the dust thy prostrate state ;
  Thy war-flag wide unfurl'd ;
And bade thee thunder at every gate
  Of the capitals of the world.

And will ye from his rest dare call
  The thunderbolt of war !
To grin and chatter around his pall,
  And scream your ' Vive la gloire ?'

Shall melo-dramic obsequies
　　His honoured dust deride ?
Forbid it, human sympathies !
　　Forbid it, Gallic pride !

What ! will no withering thought occur,
　　No thrill of cold mistrust,
How empty all this pomp and stir
　　Above a little dust ?
And will it not your pageant dim,
　　Your arrogance rebuke,
To see what now remains of him,
　　Who once the empires shook ?

Then let him rest in his stately couch
　　Beneath the open sky,
Where the wild waves dash, and the lightnings
　　　flash,
　　And the storms go wailing by.

Yes, let him rest ! such men as he
Are of no time or place ;
They live for ages yet to be,
They die for all their race.

Grace Darling's Death-bed

O WIPE the death-dews from her brow!—prop
    up her sinking head!—
And let the sea-breeze on her face its welcome
    freshness shed!
She loves to see the western sun pour glory o'er
    the deep;
And the music of the rippling waves may sing
    her into sleep.
Her heart has long, 'mid other scenes, for these
    pour'd out the sigh;
And now back to her highland home she comes
    —but comes to die.

Yes, fearful in its loveliness, that cheek's pro-
    phetic bloom ;
That lustrous eye is lighted from a world beyond
    the tomb ;
Those thin transparent fingers, that hold the
    book of prayer,
That form, which melts like summer snow, too
    plainly speak despair.
And they that tend around her bed, oft turn to
    wipe the tear,
That starts forth, as they view her thus, so fleet-
    ing, and so dear.

Not such was she that awful night when o'er
    Northumbria's foam
The shipwreck'd seaman's cry was heard with-
    in that rocky home.
Amid the pauses of the storm it loud and louder
    came,

And thrilled into her inmost soul, and nerved
    her fragile frame.
' Oh, father, let us launch the boat, and try their
    lives to save.'
' Be still, my child, we should but go to share
    their watery grave.'

Again they shriek.   ' Oh father, come, the Lord
    our guide will be :
A word from Him can stay the blast, and tame
    the raging sea.'
And lo ! at length her plea prevails ; their skiff
    is on the wave.
Protect them, gracious Heaven ! protect the
    gentle, kind, and brave !
They reach the rock, and, wond'rous sight to
    those they succour there,
A feeble girl achieving more than boldest men
    would dare !

Again, again her venturous bark bounds o'er
    the foaming tide ;
Again in safety goes and comes beneath its
    Heavenly guide.
Nor shrinks that maid's heroic heart, nor fails
    her willing hand,
'Till all the remnant of the wreck are ferried
    safe to land.
The cord o'erstrung relaxes then, and tears
    begin to fall ;—
But tears of love and praise to Him, whose
    mercy saved them all.

A deed like this could not be hid. Upon the
    wings of fame,
To every corner of our isle, flew forth Grace
    Darling's name ;
And tongues were loud in just applause, and
    bosoms highly beat,

And tributes from the great and good were
  lavished at her feet;
While she, who braved the midnight blast, and
  rode the stormy swell,
Shrank timid, trembling, from the praise that
  she had earned so well.

Why did they tempt her forth to scenes she ill
  was formed to share ?
Why bid her face the curious crowd, the ques-
  tion, and the stare ?
She did not risk her life that night to earn the
  world's applause :
Her own heart's impulse sent her forth in pity's
  holy cause.
And richly were her toils repaid, and well her
  soul content
With the sweet thought of duty done, of succour
  timely lent.

Her tender spirit sinks apace. Oh, bear the
    drooping flower
Back to its native soil again—its own secluded
    bower !
Amidst admiring multitudes, she sighs for home
    and rest :
Let the meek turtle fold her wing within her
    own wild nest ;
And drink the sights and sounds she loves, and
    breathe her wonted air,
And find with them a quiet hour for thought-
    fulness and prayer !

And she has reach'd her sea-girt home—and she
    can smile once more ;
But ah, a faint and moonlight smile, without the
    glow of yore !
The breeze breathes not as once it did upon her
    fever'd brow ;

The waves talk on, but in her breast awake no
echoes now :
For vague and flickering are her thoughts, her
soul is on the wing
For Heaven, and has but little heed for earth
or earthly thing.

'My Father, dost thou hear their shriek? dost
hear their drowning cry?'
'No, dearest, no; 't was but the scream of the
curlew flitting by.'
Poor panting, fluttering, hectic thing, thy tossings
soon will cease,
Thou art passing through a troubled sea, but to
a land of peace !
And He, who to a shipwreck'd world brought
rescue, O may He
Be near thy dying pillow now, sweet Grace, to
succour thee !

Longings for Home

STERN Britain, why a home deny
To one who loves thee well as I ?
Who woos thee with as warm a zeal
As sons for tenderest mothers feel,
Would hold to thee through good and ill,
Yet finds thee but a Step-dame still ?
Earth has for me no place of rest
So dear as thy parental breast,
No spot to which so close I cling
As to the shelter of thy wing ;
And yet thou spurn'st me from thee, yea,
Spurn'st like a prodigal away ;

Thou fling'st me suppliant from thy side,
To float a wreck upon the tide;
A boundless world at will to roam,
And sigh and think of thee and home!

Here, amidst fabled woods and streams,
The classic haunts of youthful dreams,
'Mid crumbling fanes and ruins hoary,
Rich with the hues of ancient glory;
Where every hill and every dell
Has its own stirring tale to tell,
And thoughtful pilgrims oft compare
The things that are with things that were.
Yes, here, where seems so much combined
To soothe the sense and fill the mind,
All rich, all bright, around, above,
And soft as is the voice of love,—
While at my feet in silver flakes
The evening billow gently breaks,—

I stand and muse, and o'er the sea,
My thoughts roam off to home and thee.

O what is all that earth bestows,
All that mere sense enjoys and knows,
The fairest fields, the sunniest skies,
To life's diviner charities?
Perchance this eve, so lovely here,
In my own land is bleak and drear;
And clouded skies and blustry weather,
Drive my own dear Ones close together;
And round the hearth their beaming faces
Perhaps take now their wonted places,
Each with his little social mite
To aid the general stock to-night;—
His floweret on Time's path to fling,
Or add a feather to his wing.
Oh, loved Ones, at this happy season
Of tender thought and social reason,

When hearts are full, and fancy free,
Oh, do you sometimes think of me ?—
Think of your absent wanderer, who
So fondly hangs on home and you,
And would this moment rather share
Your homely fireside converse there,
And smile with you 'neath wintry skies,
Than reign in this fair paradise !

Alas ! 't is by their loss alone
Our truest blessings oft are known.
If earth wears here a sunnier hue,
Man is the plant that thrives with you ;
A plant matured by want and toil,
And noblest oft on poorest soil.
If bleak your hills and rough your clime,
They are not rank with weeds of crime ;
The social virtues there take root,
And freedom bears her richest fruit,

While industry and skill supplies
What niggard nature else denies.
The poor man's rights have honour due,
The wronged and weak redress with you.
And boundless as yon rolling sea,
Large as the world, your charity.
Within your happy homes meanwhile
Order, and peace, and comfort smile ;
And fertile are your rugged lands
In manly minds, and hearts, and hands,
In generous aims and thoughts elate,
And all that makes men good and great.
And more than all to you is given
High intercourse with God and heaven.
Religion walking through your land
Showers down her gifts with liberal hand,
And bids the desert, as she goes,
Rejoice, and blossom like the rose.
This is thy glory, Britain ; this

Makes thy fair Island what it is—
With all its faults, in moral worth,
The Eden of this fallen earth.

Oh, gifts too lightly valued—how
My thirsty soul would prize them now!
Those hallowed Sabbaths, calm and fair,
That still well-ordered house of prayer,
The call that bids the weary come,
The ray that lights the wanderer home;
The Spirit's whisper from above,
The still small voice of truth and love.
O when, my own loved lost Ones, when
Shall we such blessings share again?
Drink of the sacred springs that flow
With balm for every want and woe,
Lift up our hearts in prayer and praise
Bequeathed from wiser, better days,

And round the Holy altar fare

On food that Angels may not share?—

When shall such joys be ours?   From high

Heard I a solemn voice reply:

'Live to your Saviour: watch and pray.

Grow in His image day by day;

And know, the Souls which thus improve

In meekness, duty, faith, and love,

Though severed in this world of pain,

In earth or Heaven shall meet again!'

NAPLES, *Christmas* 1844.

Thoughts in Weakness

PART I.—ENCOURAGEMENT

THREE mighty companies compose
　The armies of the Lord ;
Upon His love they all repose,
　And wait upon His word.
Unlike the offices they fill,
　The homage that they bring,
But one their ceaseless object still—
　To glorify their King.

The first in rank and station—they
　The bright angelic train,
Who never bowed 'neath sorrow's sway,
　Nor felt corruption's stain.

And yet they feel for man's distress,
   His every trial share,
Nor spurn the meanest services
   To help salvation's heir.

The next—a band of humbler birth,—
   But scarce of humbler place,
Who fought and bled for Christ on earth,
   And triumphed through His grace.
Their secret wrestlings, hidden life,
   To Him were not unknown :
His arm sustained them through the strife,
   And now they share His throne.

The last are they who still maintain
   The conflict here below,
Whose portion still is sin and pain,
   The danger and the foe.
They oft are foil'd, they oft despair,
   But help from high is given ;

They struggle on through faith and prayer,
  And fight their way to heaven.

And these—though poor and weak they be,
  The Saviour owns them still;
They serve Him, though imperfectly,
  And yearn to work His will.
Temptation's tide they strive to stem,
  Though faith at times burns dim,
Nor find the Lord deserting them,
  While they depend on Him.

The world, the flesh, the Evil One,
  Assault them hour by hour;
And soon must all their hopes be gone,
  If left to Nature's power.
But arm'd by Christ's own plighted word,
  When fiercest foes assail,
They meet them with the Spirit's sword,
  Nor find the weapon fail.

Oh, mighty is the power of prayer,
 The promise large and true ;
The feeblest heart need not despair
 With these to bear it through.
Though darkest clouds o'ercast the sky,
 Though wave call out to wave,
Enough to know the Saviour nigh,
 To bless, to guide, to save.

Shall flesh and blood presume to shrink
 While He vouchsafes to aid ?
Shall nature hear that voice and sink,—
 ' 'T is I, be not afraid ?'
Behold—'t is Jesus walks the deck ;
 What fears our hearts o'erwhelm ?
Can wildest waves the vessel wreck
 While He is at the helm ?

Oh, strange our courage e'er should reel
 With Him so near and kind ;

So often rescued,—yet to feel
  So trustless and so blind !
Oh, strange to know all Heaven to be
  Upon our side arrayed,
All cheering, strengthening us, and we
  By every breath dismayed !

Go ask those victors now on high
  What help'd them on to Heaven—
The very arms, they all reply,—
  To you as freely given.
Our hearts, like yours, were faint and frail,
  Our foes as hard to tame ;
But grace we found o'er all prevail.
  Oh, try and find the same !

PART II.—SUBMISSION

YET think not, O my Soul, to keep
  Thy progress on to God,
By any road less rough and steep
  Than that thy Fathers trod.
In tears and trials thou must sow
  To reap in joy and love.
We cannot find our home below,
  And hope for one above.

No—here we labour, watch, and pray,
  Our rest and peace are there—
God will not take the thorn away,
  But gives us strength to bear.
The holiest, greatest, best have thus
  In wisdom learnt to grow :
Yea, He that gave Himself for us
  Was perfected by woe.

Thou—Man of Sorrows,—Thou didst not
  The bitter cup decline.
Why should I claim a better lot,—
  A smoother path than Thine?
Thou sought'st no treasure here on earth,
  No glory 'neath the skies;
And what Thou deem'dst so little worth,
  Shall I so highly prize?

Did not reproach and wrong rain down
  Upon Thy hallowed head;
Didst Thou not strip off glory's crown
  To wear the thorns instead?
When foes reviled, didst Thou reply,
  Or render ill for ill?
Didst Thou for man bleed, faint, and die;
  And shall I falter still?

In early life to Thee I was
  Consigned by solemn vow:

Enlisted 'neath Thy Holy Cross,—
　　Shall I desert it now?
I then, 'gainst every hostile power,
　　Engaged to follow Thee;
And shall I, at the trying hour,
　　Be found the first to flee?

Thou didst not flee, O King of Love,
　　When Thou wert sorely tried;
When all men fled, and God above
　　Appeared His face to hide.
Intent that guiltless Blood to shed
　　That should for guilt atone,
The mighty wine-press Thou didst tread,
　　Unshrinking, though alone.

And shall I murmur or repine
　　At aught Thy hand may send?
To whom should I my cause resign,
　　If not to such a Friend?

Where Love and Wisdom deign to choose,
   Shall I the choice condemn ;
Or dare the medicine to refuse
   That is prescribed by them ?

Oh, small the gain when men aspire
   Their Maker to control.
He gives, perhaps, their hearts' desire,
   And leanness to their soul.
Not His to quench the smoking flax,
   Or break the bruised reed ;
Or with one pang our patience tax,
   But what he knows we need.

Yet must our steadfastness be tried,—
   Yet must our graces grow
By holy warfare. What beside
   Did we expect below?
Is not the way to Heavenly gain
   Through earthly grief and loss ?

Rest must be won by toil and pain—
The Crown repays the Cross.

As woods, when shaken by the breeze,
Take deeper, firmer root,
As winter's frosts but make the trees
Abound in summer fruit;
So every Heaven-sent pang and throe
That Christian firmness tries,
But nerves us for our work below,
And forms us for the skies.

PART III.—ACTION

Away then causeless doubts and fears
 That weaken and enthral ;
Wipe off, my Soul, thy faithless tears,
 And rise to duty's call.
How much is there to win and do.
 How much to help and cheer !
The fields are white, the labourers few ;
 Wilt thou sit 'plaining here ?

Awake, my Soul, to duty wake ;
 Go pay the debt thou ow'st.
Go forward,—and the night shall break
 Around thee as thou go'st.
A Red Sea may before thee flow,
 Egyptian hosts pursue ;

But He that bids thee onward go
  Will ope a pathway too.

Swift fly the hours, and brief the time
  For action or repose ;—
Fast flits this scene of woe and crime,
  And soon the whole shall close ;
The evening shadows deeper fall,
  The daylight dies away.
Wake, slumberer, at the Master's call,
  And work while it is day !

ROME, *April* 17, 1845.

The Czar in Rome

THE mighty Cæsar of the North
  Has entered Rome to-day.
Why peal her bells no greetings forth,
  Her crowds no tributes pay?
'Stranger, we love the great and good;
But honour not the Man of blood!'[1]

'The Man of blood! Can one so high
  Upon the lists of fame,

---

[1] In December 1845 the Emperor Nicholas of Russia, after being at Palermo and Naples, came to Rome, but met with no welcome or greeting there. His reputation had come before him, and all were indignant at his tyrannical conduct towards his Polish subjects, and his persecution of the unfortunate Roman Catholics in his dominions, whom he wished to compel to conform to the Greek Church.

Who looks and moves thus royally,
  Deserve so dark a name ?'
' Yes ! let the pining Exile tell,
The bleeding Martyr say, how well !''

While through these streets he sweeps to-day,
  The gaze of thousand eyes,
A victim of his iron sway
  In yonder convent lies,[1]
And pleads for her oppressor there.—
O King of kings, fulfil her prayer !

The soul that looks through such an eye,
  That sits on such a brow ;

---

[1] One of the unfortunate nuns from the convent of Minsk, of whom more than thirty had perished under the frightful persecutions to which they were subjected, escaped from Russia, and found her way to Rome, and was thus in a great measure the means of informing the world of the cruelties that were going on in Russia.

Must have its instincts rare and high,
  Though undeveloped now;
And moral music, strong and deep,
Among its chords must surely sleep.[1]

And who shall say, within that breast
  What throes e'en now may work?
Seems there no sign of strange unrest
  Beneath that brow to lurk?
No troubled wave to heave and roll
O'er the proud stillness of his soul?

This morn St. Peter's courts he trod,
  With stately step and stern,
Encounter'd there the man of God;—
  And how did he return?

---

[1] The Emperor Nicholas is said to be the finest-looking man in Europe.

With faltering foot, and darken'd look,
That spoke confusion and rebuke.[1]

Did some strong truth, all new and strange,
  Blest by the great ' I am,'
Drop from those reverend lips, and change
  The Lion to the Lamb?
Did pride feel there abash'd and awed,
And conscience own the voice of God?

This morn before St. Peter's shrine
  In lowly guise he knelt.
Fell on him there some Grace divine,
  With power to move and melt?

---

[1] The Emperor, the morning after his arrival, had an audience with the Pope, who appears to have spoken with great firmness and dignity upon the occasion ; and when the Emperor left his presence his face was flushed, the sweat stood on his brow, and he was evidently ill at ease.

And flew to him some wing of Love

Charged with an unction from above?[1]

While prostrate 'neath that ample dome,

   Amidst the holy dead,

Touch'd with the claims of injured Rome,

   His soul may well have said,

' Surely the Lord is in this spot,

And I, insensate, knew it not !'

Might one such feeling reach his heart,

   One thought like this prevail,

' Remember, mortal, what thou art,

   Accountable and frail !'

---

[1] After leaving the Pope, the Emperor went into St. Peter's, where he seemed awed with the majesty of the place, and fell prostrate before St. Peter's shrine, and kissed the ground. (The Greeks are worshippers of the saints, even more than the Roman Catholics.) It is even said, that there he told his attendants, that if the Roman Catholics had been persecuted in Russia, they should be so no more.

The crowns and sceptres of this earth,
Weigh'd with that thought, had little worth.

And where so well might moods like these
  Upon the spirit come
As here, where sighs the autumn breeze
  O'er desolated Rome;
Where every stone its moral brings;
Where tread we on the dust of kings!

Saw ye a shadowy hand sublime
  Write on that ruin'd wall?
Heard ye a voice, the voice of Time,
  From yon grey turret call?
'All fleets, all fades beneath the skies;
O man, be humble and be wise!'

Go forth then, King of Nations: march
  Along the Sacred way;

Stand 'neath the yet unbroken arch
 Of him who lost a day,
When he had done no generous deed ;
And wilt thou there no lesson read ?[1]

Go where the Coliseum rears
 Its sad, majestic pile,—
The pride and shame of former years :—
 Go, when the moonbeams smile,
And talk with the historic dead,
Who there have revell'd,—or have bled !

The Tyrant's trophies sink to dust ;[2]
 The Hero's still arise,

[1] A friend of mine saw the Emperor twice standing in meditative mood under the arch of Titus ; and he paid three visits to the Coliseum.

[2] It is remarked, that the only monumental remains now standing at Rome are, with one trifling exception, such as were erected to commemorate the lives and actions

True to their monumental trust,—
Lo, in the evening skies,
How freshly bright the columns shine
Of Trajan and of Antonine !

Go, then. to these mute teachers ; go !
And if, like genial rain,
Their lore upon thy heart shall flow,
Thou cam'st not here in vain ;
Nor shalt thou fail to carry home
A blessing from Eternal Rome !

---

of the most virtuous of her ancient heroes. The most perfect of these remains are the pillars of Trajan and Antoninus, the most excellent of her rulers.

Fragments

OF AN UNFINISHED POEM, ENTITLED LILLA

A FAIRY TALE

*   *   *   *   *

'T is pleasant to walk the broad sea-shore
When the soul is dark, or the heart is sore.
The waves give forth a soothing sound,
As they boom along the shelving ground;
The crispness of the salt-sea air
Breathes fresh on the fever'd brow of care:
And the waters, melting into the sky,
Send the spirit on to Eternity!
So felt Sir Rupert, as o'er the sands
That skirted his own brave house and lands

He paced, but in dark regardless mood
Of aught that there his attention woo'd.

　The sky was clear, and the sun was bright,
The blue waves danced in the shifting light,
And the foam-bells on the sand uproll'd
Like silvery fret on a floor of gold.
The far white ships sail'd stately by,
The sea-mew flitted and laugh'd on high.
But all appear'd in vain to woo
Sir Rupert's thoughts to a livelier hue.

*　　*　　*　　*　　*　　*

　From that mysterious race I 'm sprung
That lived with man, when the world was young:
But ever since envy and lust possess'd,
And ruled and sullied his own pure breast,
They have fled from earthly folly and art,
And dwell in a world of their own apart:
Hiding in Nature's secluded bowers,
Watching and tending her fruits and flowers,

Giving the blossom its scent and hue,

And the fainting leaf its drink of dew;

Spanning the shower with its bright brief arch

Leading the seasons their stately march,

Staying the storm in his fierce career.—

These are the tasks which engage us here.

Not that we less count man our friend,

Or fail on his homely wants to tend.

We note the housewife's honest cares,

And speed her labours all unawares.

We succour the mower down in the mead,

And help the ploughman to sow his seed.

We smooth the pillow where sickness lies,

And shake sweet sleep o'er the infant's eyes.

But we mingle not in man's vain affairs,

Nor darken our path with his fears and cares;

And the Court, the City, the festive hall,

We feel as strangers amidst them all.

*   *   *   *   *   *

"T is merry, 't is merry in Colmar towers,
On Rostan's hills, and in Binda's bowers,
In humble cot, and in stately hall ;
There are happy looks and hearts in all.
The cloud that hung o'er the whole is fled,
And the broad clear sun laughs out instead.
One influence sweet, one presence bright,
Has quicken'd the darkness into light.
Woman's soft smile is in Colmar found,
And it blesses and gladdens all around.
This Rupert felt, as from day to day
Lilla spread round her gentle sway ;
All, all beneath her influence grew
To a better tone, to a brighter hue.
Old Colmar's courts no longer wore
Their lorn and desolate air of yore ;
A cheerful bustle ran through the place,
Content sat beaming on every face ;
And active feet and diligent hands,

Eager to work her light commands;

And all on their various tasks intent,

At their Lady's bidding came and went.

All into life by her eye seem'd warm'd;

All to her own sweet will conform'd;

Till throughout that grim old gothic pile

Order and neatness began to smile;

And comfort lighted up there a home

That stole from the heart all wish to roam.

Nor less did improvement win its way

O'er all that around the castle lay.

The lawn, of late so rugged and wild,

Like emerald velvet now glow'd and smiled.

The walk with mosses and weeds o'erspread

Woo'd the light step o'er its gravelly bed.

Trees and shrubs that had wont to swing

Their long lank arms on the wild-wind's wing,

Were taught to conform their savage will

To the eye of taste and the hand of skill.

The fount, that long had forgot to play,
Sparkled once more in the morning ray.
The vine clung again to the elm-tree tall,
And the plum hung blue on the garden wall.—
And then the flowers, the laughing flowers,
The playmates of Lilla's earliest hours,
How did she revel among them ! how
Watch, and nurse, and enjoy them now !
Whether they grew on the wild bank, known
To the wandering bee and the lark alone ;
Or bloom'd in the garden's courtly bed,
Like orient beauties in harem bred ;
From the queen-like rose to the harebell small,
Gentle and simple she loved them all.

She loved whatever was lovely here ;
And flowers, sweet flowers, to her heart were dear.
She knew their ways, and her joy and pride
Was to gather them round her from every side.

To give them the site which themselves would
  choose,
To trim their leaves, and to match their hues ;
A staff in the weak one's hand to place,
And lift to the sun its small pale face ;
To bring the diffident out to view,
The bold to check, and the proud subdue.
Not one of them all but had its share
Of her watchful love and judicious care.
She flitted among them as if on wings,
And talk'd to them all as to living things.
And they as conscious how great their bliss,
Held up their cheeks for a passing kiss ;
Flung in her pathway their sweetest scent,
And smiled and nodded as on she went.

*　　*　　*　　*　　*　　*

They wander down to the broad sea-shore,
But not in his once dark spirit of yore.

Now, not a wild wing that across them flies,
Not a light shell in their path that lies,
Nothing in ocean, or earth, or sky,
Fails to awaken their sympathy.
Or, if the sun with his fiercer rays
Drives their steps to the woodland ways,
The squirrel is there with his chattering glee,
And the jay glad shouting from tree to tree;
And the rabbit stirring the ferns among,
And the pheasant sunning her speckled young,
Oh! nature a golden harvest yields
To all who will glean in her varied fields;
But their brightest tints her objects wear
When those that we love are nigh to share!

* * * * * *

And oh! she was rich in each social wile,
The night of its weariness to beguile!
She spoke, and mute attention hung,
Persuasion dwelt on her silver tongue;

Sweet fancies, clad in sweetest words,
Held the charm'd ear with magic chords,
And judgment clear, and taste refined,
Brought food alike to the heart and mind.
And when her favourite songs she sung,
The birds stay'd theirs ;—the soft winds hung
Entranced around her to catch the tone,
And by her music to mend their own.

* * * * * *

Each lived for each, one will, one heart;
Without a thought or a wish apart.
As streams, from opposite hills that run,
But meet in the valley, and blend in one,
Their murmurs hush'd, and their wanderings past,
Glide on together in peace at last !

* * * * * *

SONG.

Weep on ! weep on ! 't is a world of woe ;
'T is vain to expect aught else below.

The life of man has but one true tone,
From its infantile cry, to its dying groan.
Each step he takes through a land of gloom,
But carries him onward to the tomb ;
And all that he meets with as he goes
Talks to his heart of the solemn close.

Weep on ; there are many with man to weep,
The murmuring winds, and the moaning deep ;
The fading flower, and the falling dews,
And the year expiring in dolphin hues.
What says the rainbow's beautiful dream ?
Or the sunset's brief but gorgeous gleam ?
Or the summer lightning, now come, now
    gone ?—
We shine but to fade ! Weep on ! weep on !

Weep on ! it is good on this earth to weep :
If we sow in tears, we in joy may reap.

While the hopes that we madly cherish there
But pave the way to some new despair.
Pale is the young cheek's richest bloom
When it strews the path to an early tomb ;
And dim the fire of the brightest eye
When a beacon that points to mortality.

Weep on ! weep on !　　*　　*

The Complaint of Mary Magdalene

SHE sat far off,—she sat and wept,
  Heart-broken Magdalene !
Her dark and silent watch she kept
  Throughout the awful scene.
No power had she to soothe or aid,
  No hope to interpose ;
Yet love and grief her heart upstay'd
  To watch Him to the close.

'T was He, 't was He, who first the way
  Of life to her had shown ;
Had freed her soul from Satan's sway,
  And made it all His own.

'Twas He she soon had hoped to see
In Kingly glory rise,—
And now, upon the fatal Tree,
He bleeds, He faints, He dies!

And she has follow'd Him through all
His wrongs and griefs to-day,
Stood with Him in the Judgment-Hall,
Trod o'er the public way.
The scourge, the cords, the savage thorns
She shared them to the close;
Scorn'd in her outraged Master's scorns,
And bleeding in His woes.

The ponderous Cross she saw Him bear,
All fainting up the hill;
She saw them nail Him on it there
With unrelenting skill;

She heard their wild and withering cry
  As He aloft was swung,
The gaze of every flashing eye,
  The scoff of every tongue !

No angel comes, on wings of love,
  His sinking soul to cheer ;
The very Heavens seem shut above,
  And Mercy fails to hear ;
Despised, deserted, crush'd, and awed,
  He hangs upon the tree,
And cries in vain, ' My God, My God,
  Hast Thou forsaken me ?'

O trying scene for woman's eye !
  And yet she braved it all ;
The struggle and the agony,
  The wormwood and the gall,—

Though earth beneath in horror shook,
　Though Heaven its light withdrew,
And sterner hearts the awe partook,
　Yet woman braved it through.

She sat far off—she sat and wept,
　Heart-broken Magdalene !
Her dark and silent watch she kept
　Throughout the trying scene !
She sank not when His head He bow'd,
　She bore His dying groan—
Till pass'd away the sated crowd,
　And left her there alone !

The shades of evening round her head
　Now gather'd thick and fast ;
And forth her burthen'd spirit fled
　In louder woe at last.

Upon the ear of silent night
   Her plaintive murmurs broke,
And sorrow seem'd to grow more light
   As thus she wept and spoke.—

'And is all over? Can it be
   That they have had their will?
Thou hanging, Lord, on yonder tree,
   And we surviving still?
Is this to be the course and close
   Of all Thy conflicts past?
A brief, dark path through wrongs and woes
   To such a death at last?

' Yes, past all reach of ill Thou art,—
   I see no living sign;
And, oh that this sad struggling heart
   Were now as still as Thine!

I groan—Thou canst not heed my groan,
    Nor answer when I plain.—
Ah! I shall never hear the tone
    Of that blest voice again.

'O hallow'd head! compell'd to bow
    Beneath unnumber'd scorns;
O dear, dishonour'd, glorious brow,
    Now crush'd beneath the thorns;
O eyes, where Heaven seem'd once to reign,
    Can ye grow glazed and dim?
O Death—by Him for others slain,
    Canst thou have power o'er Him?

'How couldst thou, brutal soldier, dare
    To pierce that breast divine?—
There never dwelt a feeling there
    But love to thee and thine.

How could ye harm one tender limb
  Of His, ye murderous crew,
And know, that while ye tortured Him
  He pray'd for you, for you?

'It must be right, I feel it must,
  Though all is darkness now;—
Lord, teach my trembling heart to trust,
  And help my will to bow!
'T is hard upon that Cross to gaze,
  Nor feel the Tempter's power.
O God! sustain me through the maze
  Of this mysterious hour!

'Yes! mystery o'er the whole doth hang,
  To be unravelled still.
Who could on Him inflict a pang
  Without the Sufferer's will?

He, whom the slumbering dead have heard,
  Whose voice the winds could tame,
Could not He crush them with a word
  If such had been His aim?

'But I remember well, when hope
  Seem'd most our hearts to cheer,
What hints and warnings He would drop
  Of pain and trial near.
He, doubtless, was intent to give
  A lesson here from high;
And as He taught us how to live,
  Would teach us now to die!

'Yet surely 't was a loftier task
  That drew Him from the skies,
And ne'er could mere example ask
  So dire a sacrifice;—

And surely these were all to tend
At last to brighter bliss,
Not prematurely here to end
In double night like this.

'All prophecy proclaims a time
When Satan's rule shall cease,
When Earth shall pass from woe and crime
To endless love and peace,—
When Death and Hell with all their hosts
Shall quail before their Lord,
And more than was in Adam lost
Shall be in Christ restored.

'Yes, Lord of lords, and King of kings,
For such Thou art to me,
My soul through doubt and darkness clings
With trembling faith to Thee,—

I feel some brighter morn shall yet
  Our shatter'd hopes surprise,
And glory's sun, that now is set,
  Again in glory rise.

'The great Messiah still Thou art,
  Confirm'd by every sign ;
And this may all be but a part
  Of some sublime design.
What God ordains must needs be best,—
  What He permits is right ;
On Him, on Him my soul I rest,
  And wait for further light.

'One mournful task is left me too,—
  Thy dear remains to tend ;
With honours due Thy bier to strew,
  And watch Thee to the end.

Then let me to Thy lifeless clay
    Still sadly, fondly cling,
And wait, and weep, and hope, and pray
    For what the day may bring.'—

She said, and seem'd to ease her breast
    In these complaints and prayers;
Then rose, and went to seek the rest,
    And mingle tears with theirs.
She went the spices to provide,
    His last sad rites to pay,—
Then by the tomb sat down and sigh'd,
    'Oh, when will it be day?'

January 1st, 1847

WHAT solemn footfall smote my startled ear !

Heard I the step of the departing year ?

Saw I her shadowy form flit slowly by,

To join her sisters in eternity ?—

Sweeping down thither, as the autumn's blast

Sweeps summer's leaves, the records of the past,

The joys and griefs, the bustle and the strife,

The shadows and realities of life ?

Hear me, stern daughter of old Time, O hear !—

Is there no plea may stay thy strong career ?

O pause in pity ! pause, and to my prayer

Grant a brief converse with the things that were—

I know the retrospect has much to pain,

Much to be mended could all come again ;

Still, without one last look we must not sever,
Sad is the word that bids to part for ever!
Beam, then, again on me, dear, kindly faces,
And smile your best, old times and well-known
    places;
Bright looks, soft tones, high thoughts,` and
    fancies fair,
Return, return, and be what once you were!
All that was precious in the year that's past,—
Too sweet to lose, too beautiful to last—
Sunshine, and song, and fragrance, things that
    threw
O'er life's dull path a brighter tint and hue;
Hopes realized, desires fulfill'd;—success
Crowning long toils; the burthens of distress
Lighten'd, Will subjugated, Self denied,
Ills overcome by long endurance, Pride
Taught to be greatly humble,—all that wakes
The approving voice of conscience, all that makes

Heaven's windows open o'er us, converse sweet,
And sweeter meditation ; all,—all fleet
Back into being.—Burst oblivion's chain,
And be awhile realities again !—

Blest be the powers that can the past restore ;—
They come, they come, warm breathing as of
  yore !
I hear remember'd voices, seem to dwell
Once more with forms I 've known and loved
  so well.
Distinct, beyond my fondest hopes, they rise,
The shadows dimming the realities.
Beautiful witcheries ! Oh, would I might
Hold them thus ever, durable as bright !
But, like the splendours of a sunset sky,
E'en while I gaze their glories wane and die,
And, as they fade, uprising in their rear
A host of darker verities appear ;

Sorrows and sins of various shade and hue,
That claim their notice in the year's review.
And shall they be rejected? shall my eyes
Be shut to life's too stern realities?
And shall the records of the past be seen,
Not as they were, but as they should have been?
No! small the gain and brief the joy that lives
In the poor dreams such self-delusion gives;
And honest conscience scorns to take a tone,
Or speak a flattering language not her own;
And wherefore seek to bribe her, wherefore fear
Her rough but salutary voice to hear,
When every warning, now rejected, grows
To overwhelming thunder at the close?

The close! the close!   How like a death-knell
    seems
That solemn word to wake me from my dreams!
One little year, yea, less than one like this,
May bring me to the close of all that is.

Far down Time's chequered stream I 've
    voyaged on,
And seen my fellows drop off, one by one ;
And now the widening waters seem to near
Eternity's dark ocean ; on my ear
Sound the deep heavings of that shoreless sea,
And awe my soul into solemnity !
Darkling I hover round the world to come,
And voices thence are heard to call me home ;
And stretching on into the dread expanse,
I fain would lift the curtain, and advance.
One little step, I know, would bear me through,
And give the secrets of the dead to view ;
But till that step is taken, mortal sense,
Ask as it may, gets no response from thence.
Thought may at times, when all around me sleep,
Launch sounding forth into that silent deep ;
But without star to guide or light to cheer,
Soon back to land my trembling course I steer.

E'en bold Conjecture onward fears to fare,
And Reason shrinks to find no footing there ;
Till conscious Nature, baffled and o'er-awed,
Sinks suppliant on the Mercy of her God,
Turns from self-confidence to faith and prayer,
Clings to His Word, and finds her refuge there.

Thrice happy we, not left to grope our way
From truth to truth, by Nature's feeble ray,
Where one false step were ruin.   Happier still
Our wills conforming to the Heavenly Will ;
Ready, as God may prompt, to think, and feel,
And take His impress, as the wax the seal ;
At His blest feet content to sit and learn,
Or walk by faith, till faith to sight shall turn ;
Beneath the Saviour's cross to stand and scan
All He has done, and all He claims from man ;
Learn from His life, and on His death repose,
And grow in love and duty to the close.

On the year's threshold, on the narrow strand
That parts the past and future, here I stand,
Without control o'er either : one is flown
Beyond recal ;—a dark and dread unknown,
The other stretches onward,—what to be,
Seen but by Him who fills Eternity.
The present, and scarce that, is still my own ;—
Oh, be it consecrate to Heaven alone !
Be mine, while all things shift and change around,
To cleave to Him in whom no change is found,
To rest on the Immutable, to cling
Closer and closer 'neath the Almighty wing ;
His voice in all its varied tones to hear,
And in all aspects feel Him ever near ;
Be mine with Him to walk, on Him depend,—
Then, come what may, it all to good must tend !

Rome.

The Poet's Plea

DEAL gently with the poet.   Think that he
   Is made of finer clay than other men,
And ill can bear rough handling; and while we,
   Of sturdier natures, laugh'd at laugh again,
And self-complacently shake off
The world's unmerited contempt and scoff—
As easily as from his scaly side
Leviathan shakes off the drippings of the tide;—
Not so the poet.   On his keener sense
Light harms smite often with an edge intense.
A stony look, a lip of scorn, may crush
His young aspirings; chill the stir and flush
Of waking inspiration; and control
Down into common-place the darings of his soul.

Lightly his spirit touch !
The lyre is delicate ; the chords are fine ;
And fine must be the finger, that from such
    Wins melody divine.
The strings, that gentler skill to music wakes,
    A clash impetuous breaks.
And images, that, in the musing mind,
As in a placid lake, lie mirrored and defined,
If ruffling winds along the surface stray,
Scatter'd and broken, pass like rack away.
Stored thoughts and treasured feelings, that in
    turn
Were ready to leap forth, and breathe, and burn
In verse, as fancy called them, once dispersed,
Bide, like the Sibyl's leaves, unscanned and
    unrehearsed.

    And, Desolater, who shall say
Of what thy rashness may have 'reft mankind ?

Take the sweet poetry of life away,
    And what remains behind?
Oh, who his seventy years would delve and plod,
And tug through life's dull tide the weary oar,
Were all his heritage what earth's poor clod
    Can yield, and nothing more?
Perhaps the Poet had that moment caught
Some   hallowed   truth,   some   spirit-stirring
    thought,
That—like the wakening of a trumpet blast,—
From age to age might thrillingly have pass'd.
Perhaps some happy fancy, some fair dawn
Of beauty, on his mind may just have shone;—
Some touch of holy tenderness, whose spell
Might melt and mend all hearts whereon it fell.
He was, perhaps, aloft among the stars,—
Perhaps beyond them; leaning on the bars,
    The golden bars, that Heaven enclose,
    List'ning the music that within—

A vocal glory, fell and rose

From lips of chaunting seraphin ;

Intent to carry down from thence

All that could enter mortal sense,

Dull'd as it is by sin ;—

And thou didst call him down from tasks like
these,

To mix with common life's poor, tame formalities !

Go, Man of earth, and do thy work ! obey

Thy five good senses !   Traffic, drudge, design !

To small civilities due homage pay !—

The Poet has his province, and thou thine.

He dwells within a sphere thou canst not enter,

Nearer the throne, fast by the mighty centre ;

And hears what cannot reach the unchasten'd ear

Of those who stand outside, among the million
here.

To thee and thine belong the Gentile courts,

To which the uncircumcised crowd resorts.

He finds admittance to the inmost shrine,

Which none can hope to reach till led by hands
    divine.

Keep then thy place.   Thou hast good work to
    do ;

Not they alone the temple service share

Who tend the altar.   Those are needful too,

Who hew the wood and draw the water there.

The daily drudgery of life demands

A due relay of honest heads and hands ;

They have their use ; shall have their pay besides.

The world is just, and for her own provides.

To thrive in pelf, in pomp and place to shine ;

These are her gifts, and these shall, Man of
    earth, be thine.

But trench not on the Poet's charter'd rights,

He walks his own domain with haughty brow :

His heavenly communings, his eagle flights
    Are not for such as thou.

High thoughts, warm feelings, the perennial spring
Of inward gladness, rapture's thrill and glow,
The heart in flower, the fancy on the wing,—
    Thou must not hope to know.
These are the Poet's dower.   Of these possest,
He smiles, and bids earth's minion take the rest!

But spare, ye men of fact, ye sapient band,
With critic lore, our desperate ears to stun.
Carp not at that you do not understand;
Nor spend your shafts in shooting at the sun.
The rich creations, which the Poet flings
In rainbow radiance from his passing wings,
You may not duly relish, rightly scan;
Yet think, wise sirs, there may be those who can;
And kill not his fine frenzies with your frown,
Nor to your standard seek to dwarf him down.
You prize the useful.   Be it so.   Yet tell,
In what consists this useful?   The All-wise,

In furnishing the world in which we dwell,

Stints not His gifts to mere necessities;

Nor deems it waste to tint the bird's bright wing,

   Yea, give him voice to sing;

To beautify the flower, and to its bloom

   To superadd perfume.

Things need not be fantastic nor unreal

   Because they are ideal.

Nay, every object in this world of dreams

   Is what to each it seems.

And that, which quickens into action all

Of good in man, that has survived the fall,

Refines each baser sense, and helps to call

From all that is, the good, the beautiful;

That bids Experience half her ills withhold,

And turns whate'er it touches into gold;—

Can that be useless? that, whose hallowing leaven

Imparts to this poor world whate'er it has of

   Heaven?

O empty Cavillers! why not assign
New laws to Nature, teach the stars to shine?
Soar through the clouds, proud gazer at the sun,
And leave the owls and bats at noonday to doze on!

Yet not the worldly, nor the dull alone
Refuse Heaven's favoured one his homage due:
Minds of a larger grasp and loftier tone
    Oft wrong the Poet too.
    Oh, the half-hearted praise,
The chilling toleration, men can give
To powers, that mortals from the dust can raise
    Among the gods to live!
    Who shall the boons declare
With which the Poet sows our fallen earth?
The holy thoughts, and sweet emotions there,
    That owe to him their birth?
    High sentiments, now grown
Familiar household terms mankind among,

Are oft but sparklets of the soul, once thrown

From some poetic tongue;

Rich emanations of some pregnant mind,

Bright gems of thought in happy words enshrined;

That lend to common life a higher tone,

And touch within men's hearts, chords to them-

selves unknown.

And shall the Poet, like a kindled torch,

For us and ours in self-devotion burn,

And taunts that blister, and rebukes that scorch

Be dealt him in return?

Shall all his thoughtful toil,

His midnight watchings, solitude, and pain,

Ask the cheap meed of one approving smile,

And ask in vain?

Shall we prefer to sit

In cold, stern dignity, in Censure's chair,

When we with him on social wing might flit

Through ocean, earth, and air?

When we might rise and reign
In each high privilege to genius given,
Bright, living links of the electric chain
Connecting earth with Heaven?
O senseless choice! that frowns and stands apart,
When both might sweetly mingle, heart with heart!
O poor exchange, the critic's carps and sneers,
For poetry's full soul, her raptures, and her tears!

Make large allowance, then, for Nature's child;
School him not tamely down to rule and line.
Let the fine Savage roam his native wild;
Nor fetter Fancy's chartered libertine.
The stale observances to dulness dear,—
O chide not, if beyond their pale he rove,
And rise from Lar and the Penates here,
To walk the Heavens with Jove.
Be his to pierce the wild wood's tangled maze,
And find or force new by-paths of his own.

The fruits are gathered by the beaten ways ;
    The flowers are trampled down.
    Be his aloft to soar
Within the winnow of Archangel's wing,
And hear beneath his feet the thunder's roar,
    And the grim whirlwinds sing.
    Within the hearts of men,
Be his each secret chamber to unbar,
And drag the struggling passions from their den,
    To yoke them to his car.
Free, let him range the globe from land to land,
And some new lore from every object win :
Or by the flood of ages thoughtful stand,
And hear earth's Empires one by one drop in.
Calm let him sit by nature's mighty wheel,
To watch her workings, and her ways reveal,
Or launch abroad her silent depths to sound,
And bring up wonders for the world around.
Grand his ambitions !   Be his scope as grand !

They only greatly do, who greatly dare ;
Why snatch the club from Hercules's hand
    To place the distaff there ?
No ! let him dally with the lightnings ; fling
Forth, if he will, upon the tempest's wing ;
Ride the careering billow without rein,
And stroke with playful hand its foamy mane ;
And scorning by the servile shore to creep,
Forth let him steer to seek new worlds across
    the deep.

Yet should the worst befal, should wrongs assail,
Should envy harass, or indifference chill,
Should evil days and evil tongues prevail,
Be strong, O genius ! much is left thee still.
The bypath through the meads is warm and sweet ;
Soft evening breezes from the orchards play ;
Crush'd herbs give out their odours 'neath thy feet,
And flashing brooks dance by thee all the way.

The small shrill people of the grass
Chirp welcomes as they see thee pass ;
The flowers unlock their hearts, and thence
Breathe odorous secrets forth to thy quick sense.
Dryads and Fauns in woodland spaces,
Push through the leaves their laughing faces ;
And bending boughs to thee make suit,
And to thy hand present their tributary fruit.
Thine are the living fountains,
That down the rocks in liquid silver run ;
Thine are the giant mountains,
That lift their broad green shoulders to the
sun.
The clouds that sail the summer sky,
Or o'er their shadows anchor high ;
The stars that round the matron moon
People with glory the blue vault of June,
All, all, are thine ! From off her ample breast,
Sweet Nature, flinging wide her folded vest,

Gives thee her very self unveil'd to see,

And freely talks her inmost soul to thee.

Yea, and should these all fail thee, still thou hast

Thy solace ; hast thy white, auspicious days,

When thoughts—like showering meteors, bright

    and fast,

Flash on thy soul, self-clad in aptest phrase.

Thou hast thy glorious visions of the night,

Mysterious converse with the mighty dead ;

Angelic visitants, from realms of light,

Ascending and descending o'er thy head.

    There may be toil.   While here,

Man in his sweat, his daily bread must eat ;

Yet faint not.   There is much thy work to cheer,

The very pains of poetry are sweet,

    The streams which others' thirst supply

    Shall not be to their owner dry ;

And precious draughts from thence shall bless,

And stay thy spirit through the wilderness.

A light shall guide thee better than the rules
The world employs to school her knaves and fools.

A happy instinct bears the Poet through ;
And while he speaks and writes, he lives the
      Poet too.

And as thou sitt'st and singest all apart,
Feeling it recompense enough to vent
The throbbing pulses of a pent-up heart,
And make the soul's mute yearnings eloquent ;
      Those Argosies of thought and rhyme
      Thou launchest on the stream of Time,
      Floating to unborn generations down,
Shall blessings bear to them, and to thyself
      renown.
      That which is truly noble cannot die !
      Eternal as its hallow'd course on high !
      Heroes and Conquerors have their day ;
      Kings with their Empires pass away.
      Things, which to marble we intrust,
      Shall with it moulder into dust.

But one true flash of living mind,
At Heaven's own altar kindled and refined,
    Shall travel, like a beacon light,
    From intellectual height to height,
Unquenched, unquenchable! Seas cannot
      drown,
Mountains o'erwhelm it, legions tread it down;
A moment lost, 't is sure again to rise,
And lead, from strength to strength, still on-
      ward to the skies.

Yet think, O mortal, think, while thus endow'd
With more than mortal privilege and power,
Think how they lift thee o'er the ignoble crowd,
Who walk by sense, and live but for the hour.
    Gifts that have had their birth
Beyond the everlasting hills on high,
Sent down to dwell awhile in hearts on earth,
Should still tend upward to their native sky.

Husks, that the swine do eat,

Earth's bursting bubbles, must not thee delight,

With Heaven's own Manna falling at thy feet,

And Canaan's promised glories full in sight.

No! be it thine to rise

In noble scorn of every meaner thing,

Self-buoyant, like the bird of paradise

That sleeps and wakes for ever on the wing.

The vestal fire must not be left to wane,

Nor lightly desecrate to use profane.

Thou walk'st this earth the delegate of Heaven ;

And much shall be required where much is given.

Not that the tone need always be sublime ;

The light and graceful have their place and time.

But for the loose, the impious, or the base,

Exists no privilege of time or place.

Oh, scorn them, scorn them! To thyself be true !

Breathe not a thought thou e'er shalt wish un-
    said ;

Nought that may haunt and sadden life's review,
Or cast a shadow o'er thy dying bed.
Thine is a lofty mission.   Nothing less
Than God to glorify, and Man to bless;
To raise poor grovelling Nature from the mire,
To give her wings, and teach her to aspire;
To nurse heroic moods; meek worth to cheer;
To dry on sorrow's cheek the trembling tear;
And still be ready, let who will deride,
To take the lists on injured Virtue's side.

      This is thy calling.   Tasks like these
Claim and repay the soul's best energies.
Nor need'st thou fear, while thus employed,
That life should seem a burthen or a void.
Joys shall be thine, Man makes not, nor unmakes;
Cheer, which the fickle world nor gives nor takes;
Unhoped-for streams that in the desert rise,
And sunshine bursting through the cloudiest
      skies!

From light to light thy steps shall tend,
Thy prospects ever brightening to the end ;
Thy soul acquiring as it goes
The tone and feelings that befit the close.
Such path, O gifted one, be thine to tread !
And when the Judge of quick and dead
To each His sentence shall assign,
' Well done, thou faithful servant !' shall be thine !
And thou shalt rise the tasks of Heaven to share,
Join the blest choir, and feel no stranger there.
And ' power and honour to the Lamb' shall seem
To thee no new and uncongenial theme.
The strains, to which thy earthly powers were
given,
Shall be renew'd and perfected in Heaven ;
And more than e'er blest Poet's dream, shall be
The Poet's portion there throughout eternity !

ROME, *March* 1847.

To a Field-flower

Found beside a favourite arbour early in Spring

Hail, lovely harbinger of Spring !
    Hail, little, modest Flower !
Fann'd by the tempest's icy wing,
    Dash'd by the hoary shower.
Thy balmy breath, thy soften'd bloom
    Was ever welcome here ;
But at this hour of Wintry gloom
    Thy smile is doubly dear.

The storm that o'er thy mossy bed,
    Subdues the towering tree,
Flies harmless o'er thy shelter'd head,
    And wears no scowl for thee ;

But resting in security,
    Thou teachest haughty souls
The blessings of obscurity,
    Where ruin's whirlwind rolls.

The tulip flaunts in rich array;
    The rose is passing sweet;
But, ah! with Summer's golden day,
    Their gaudy charms retreat:
But while the lingering Winter lowers,
    And saddens all the green,
Thou, herald mild of brighter hours
    Thy soothing smiles are seen.

Thy gems are strew'd in every place,
    On every bank they fling
An early wreath, with artless grace
    Around the brows of Spring;

In woodland wilds, in gardens gay,
     In vale, on mountain drear;
The first to meet the sunny ray,
     And hail the waking year.

Oh! thou art Nature's fondest care,
     The foster-child of Spring!
The virgin twines thee in her hair
     To dance at village ring.
The bee, in thy soft bosom, stays
     His winglet's wild career;
The lark his morning song of praise
     Pours in thy dewy ear!

Dear, little, timorous, gentle flower,
     Sweet pilgrim of the storm,
Still, still beneath my sheltering bower
     Recline thy paly form!

No plundering grasp, no heedless bruise,
Shall harm one bud of thine :
And gaudier sweets while others choose,
The Primrose shall be mine.

BALLOW-WATER, *April* 27, 1812.

Song

Sweetest daughter of the year,
Smiling June, I hail thee here.
Hail thee with thy skies of blue,
Days of sunshine, nights of dew.
Hail thee with thy songs and flowers,
Balmy air, and leafy bowers,
Bright and fragrant, fresh and clear,
Smiling June, I hail thee here.

Yet, sweet June, it is not these
Perfumed gales and whispering trees
Blossoms shed with liberal hand,
Like a star-shower o'er the land,

Waves at rest and woods in tune ;
'T is not these, delicious June,
Gives thee such a charm for me,
Moves me thus to welcome thee.

'T is that Agnes on thy skies
Open'd first her brighter eyes ;
That the flower of all thy flowers
Woke to life within thy bowers ;
Gave thy charms a higher tone,
Lent thee honours not thy own ;
And for this, thy brightest boon,
Take thy tribute, lovely June.

1816.

May Flowers

Sweet Babes, dress'd out in flowers of May,
And fair and innocent as they :
A lovely type in them we see
Of what you are, and what must be.
Like them you rise, like them you bloom,
Like them you hasten to the tomb.
Ye human flowers, smile on, smile on !
Your hours of bliss will soon be gone.

Soon manhood with its cares and crimes
Shall cloud these early sunny times,
And call you from your sports and flowers
To passions and pursuits like ours.

And what are all that men pursue
But flowrets, gather'd flowrets, too?
Howe'er they tempt, howe'er they please,
More fleeting and less fair than these.

Enjoyments, honours, talents, sway,
Wealth, beauty, all must pass away;
A cloud must come across their sky,
A frost but nips them, and they die.
One flower alone, when all are gone,
Shall bloom for aye unfading on—
'T is Grace—the treasure seek and prize;
It grows to Glory in the skies.

1817.

𝔄. 𝔐. 𝔐. 𝔏.

DIED FEBRUARY 1821, AGED ONE MONTH

A few brief moons the Babe who slumbers
    here
Smiled on her parents, and that innocent smile
Was daylight to their eyes. They thought her
    fair,
And gentle, and intelligent, and dared
To lean their hearts upon her. There are ways
And looks of hers that long will dwell with
    them,
And there are bright anticipations held,
How fondly and feelingly resign'd !
Her very helplessness endear'd her to them,
And made her more their own.—But this is
    done :–

The wintry wind pass'd o'er the opening flower,
And nipp'd it in the bud—and it is gone.

Still there is comfort left.   It still is joy
That they can lift their weeping eyes to Heaven,
And think that one of theirs is settled there ;
Can know, beyond the shadow of a doubt,
That she is safe with Him who bears the lambs
Within His bosom, and, no longer Babe
But Angel, now beholds her Father's face,
And shares the fulness of eternal joy.

Sweet Spirit, since now the ministry of love
From God to erring man is thine, O draw
The souls of those who loved thee to the place
Where thou art gone before them ; make them feel
That earth is not their home ; O fix their thoughts

On Heaven, on Him who once on earth took up
Babes such as thou, and blessed them, and
    bade all
Who look'd for Heaven become like Babes,—
    like thee,
Pure, innocent, lowly, loving, and new-born.

Hark! round the God of Love

Hark! round the God of Love
    Angels are singing!
Saints at His feet above
    Their crowns are flinging.
And may poor children dare
    Hope for acceptance there,
Their simple praise and prayer
    To His throne bringing?

Yes! through adoring throngs
    His pity sees us,
'Midst their seraphic songs
    Our offering pleases.

And Thou who here didst prove
To babes so full of love,
Thou art the same above,
Merciful Jesus !

Not a poor sparrow falls
But Thou art near it.
When the young raven calls,
Thou, Lord, dost hear it.
Flowers, worms, and insects share,
Hourly Thy guardian care—
Wilt Thou bid us despair?
Lord, can we fear it?

Lord, then thy mercy send
On all before Thee !
Children and children's friend,
Bless, we implore Thee !

Lead us from grace to grace,
On through our earthly race,
Till all before Thy face
Meet to adore Thee!

Abide with me

*"Abide with us: for it is toward evening, and the day is far
spent."*—ST. LUKE xxiv. 29

ABIDE with me!   Fast falls the eventide ;
The darkness deepens : Lord, with me abide !
When other helpers fail, and comforts flee,
Help of the helpless, O abide with me !

Swift to its close ebbs out life's little day ;
Earth's joys grow dim ; its glories pass away :
Change and decay in all around I see ;
O Thou, who changest not, abide with me !

Not a brief glance I beg, a passing word,
But as Thou dwell'st with Thy disciples, Lord,

Familiar, condescending, patient, free,
Come, not to sojourn, but abide, with me !

Come not in terrors, as the King of kings ;
But kind and good, with healing in Thy wings :
Tears for all woes, a heart for every plea.
Come, Friend of sinners, and thus bide with
   me !

Thou on my head in early youth didst smile,
And, though rebellious and perverse meanwhile,
Thou hast not left me, oft as I left Thee.
On to the close, O Lord, abide with me !

I need Thy presence every passing hour.
What but Thy grace can foil the Tempter's
   power ?
Who like Thyself my guide and stay can be ?
Through cloud and sunshine, O abide with me !

I fear no foe with Thee at hand to bless :

Ills have no weight, and tears no bitterness.

Where is death's sting? where, grave, thy victory?

I triumph still, if Thou abide with me.

Hold Thou Thy cross before my closing eyes :

Shine through the gloom, and point me to the
    skies :

Heaven's morning breaks, and earth's vain
    shadows flee.

In life and death, O Lord, abide with me !

BERRYHEAD, *September* 1847.

EDINBURGH: T. CONSTABLE,
PRINTER TO THE QUEEN, AND TO THE UNIVERSITY.